KENNETH A KIDD

THEY'RE HERE!!
ALIENS AMONG US

They're Here!!: Aliens Among Us
Copyright © 2023 by Kenneth A Kidd

ISBN: 978-1639457830 (hc)
ISBN: 978-1639457816 (sc)
ISBN: 978-1639457823 (e)

All rights reserved. No part of this publication may be reproduced, distributed, or transmitted in any form or by any means, including photocopying, recording, or other electronic or mechanical methods, without the prior written permission of the publisher or author, except in the case of brief quotations embodied in critical reviews and certain other noncommercial uses permitted by copyright law.

The views expressed in this book are solely those of the author and do not necessarily reflect the views of the publisher, and the publisher hereby disclaims any responsibility for them.

Writers' Branding
(877) 608-6550
www.writersbranding.com
media@writersbranding.com

Chapter 1

It was 3:30 a.m., and Lyman Shore was lying awake in his one-bedroom condo, staring up at the darkness. At forty-two, he took pride in keeping his five foot eleven frame in good shape, working out daily to keep the muscles hard and the mind sharp. *I wonder what the fuck this day might bring,* he thought. *Has it really been only two weeks since my old high school friend Drake Borden had called and made that strange request? It seemed a lifetime ago.*

"What the hell was that?" he said to himself as he bolted upright in the bed. He felt it more than heard it, a presence approaching from the kitchen stealthily in total darkness. He reached under the pillow for his Glock 17 as he silently swung his legs off the bed and slid down on his knees to the floor while taking aim at the door leading to the kitchen. Staring into total darkness, he sensed the slightest change in the movement of the air around him and knew the door was opening ever so slowly.

If whoever it is has night goggles, I'll be toast once that door opens, he thought, and he squeezed off two quick rounds as he dropped and rolled to his left. The sound of the two shots bursting through the total silence was deafening, but he still heard the opening door slam against the wall as the figure, dressed in black, fell to the floor in front of him. Hopping more than jumping onto the man's back and landing with his knees just below the shoulders, he felt down his arms to find the silenced Sig Sauer still grasped in his dead right hand. *Did I ask what the fuck this day might bring?* he thought.

Lyman was the third of three sons his parents would have. Raised in the small rural town of Westport in Southeastern Massachusetts, he had a "leave it to beaver" upbringing. No domestic violence, child abductions, or violent crime existed in his world as he would play outside with friends until darkness started to fall and then ride his bike home for dinner with the family. They would watch some television or play games and off to bed for a good night's sleep before getting up for school the next day. With two older brothers, he always wanted to be older like them. Little did he realize how great those years were until many years later. He was just nine years old when his father moved the family to San Antonio following a job transfer.

The dead man lying on his bedroom floor was a Caucasian male who looked to be in his early to midthirties. I say "looked to be" because there was no identification on him. "Why am I not surprised?" Lyman said aloud to no one.

Lyman Shore was a nineteen-year-old PFC with the First Armored Division's First Squadron, First Cavalry on December 31, 1995, when he crossed the Sava River from Croatia into BosniaHerzegovina. As the gunner in the Abrams M1A2 tank, it was his job to scour the approaching countryside as they arrived in-country to begin their mission. For the next year, he would experience firsthand the cluster fuck that was the former Yugoslavia—Serbs, Croats, Slovenes, Muslims, Catholics, and Russian Orthodox Jews taking turns slaughtering one another. Now the US Army put twenty thousand troops under NATO control into Operation Joint Endeavor. Their mission? To enforce a cease-fire, separate the warring factions, and supervise boundaries along zones of separation in accordance with the Dayton Peace Accords. He would never again in his life witness firsthand just how cruel and sinister mankind could be. Mass graves and indiscriminate killing of entire families—that experience changed him forever.

Brett Boyer shared that M1A2 tank with Lyman as his ammunition loader. That was twenty-two years ago, and Brett had since inherited his father's funeral business. His iPhone rang with the soundtrack from *A Few Good Men* as he worked on the finishing touches for a newly departed client. *Who would be calling at three forty-five in the morning?* he thought. *Perhaps a domestic violence death after a drunken husband comes home with the smell of another woman all over him and confronts a hostile wife,* he pondered as he took the call. "Perpetual Memories Funeral Home."

"What's up, ammo man?" Lyman said.

"Hey, Shore." (He always called him by his last name.) "How's everything in the world of a deputy US Marshal?"

Lyman and Brett graduated high school together in San Antonio, Texas, in 1994 and, a year later, decided to enlist in the Army under the buddy plan, which allowed them to serve together for their three-year enlistment. Upon discharge, they returned to San Antonio, where Lyman took advantage of the GI Bill to get a degree in criminal justice from UTSA and Brett started learning about the funeral business from his father.

"I need a favor, old buddy. How about I buy you breakfast?"

At one thirty the following morning, Brett was at Lyman's condo, helping him transport the nameless intruder under the cover of darkness to the funeral home. Lyman had explained the situation to Brett over breakfast at the IHOP off Loop 410 near the airport the morning before, and Brett had gone over to Lyman's condo that afternoon to prepare the body for transport. Getting local authorities involved in this was not a viable option. He brought the hearse with him because loading a body into Lyman's canary-yellow Camaro was not a possibility.

"You owe me big-time," said Brett as he closed the heavy crematorium door and flipped the switch on Lyman's uninvited visitor.

"Anything you need, anytime, ammo man. I'm your go-to guy," Lyman promised.

"I was never here."

And at 3:00 a.m., Lyman quietly left the funeral home and walked back to his car. It was time to give Drake Borden a visit. He decided he would drive on up to Austin and park outside the governor's office and wait for Drake to arrive. If he wasn't there by nine, he would go in to see what information he could get by using his deputy marshal ID. Somebody just tried to kill him, and all his subsequent calls to Drake had gone to voice mail with none returned. He was going to find out what the hell was going on before anyone else decided to give him a late-night visit.

CHAPTER 2

Drake Borden lived in Austin, Texas, where he worked in the governor's office as the communications director. It was his job to see that Governor William T. Jacobs was viewed in the most positive light by all the citizens of the great state of Texas. Before that call came two weeks ago, he had not heard from him since he was a senior in high school.

"Hello," Lyman had answered.

"Hello, Lyman? This is Drake Borden calling from the governor's office here in Austin. How the hell are you, old friend?"

"Drake, it's been a long time, buddy. So now you're a big shot in the governor's office. What's up?"

"Well, I have a little bit of a problem up here, and you're the only one I know in the Marshals office."

"Okay, you've piqued my interest. Lay it on me," Lyman replied.

"You have a gentleman by the name of Charles 'Chuck the Mutilator' Mankewitz in the witness protection program. We need to talk to him," he said.

"Drake, that is a bit problematic from where I stand. There is a reason why they call it witness protection, and what you're asking is way above my pay grade. I would need a lot more information before I could take this to my superiors."

"Well, Lyman, just tell your boss that the request came from the governor himself, that lives are at stake, and time is of the essence. I'm not at liberty to say any more at this time."

"I'll see what I can do, Drake, but no promises."

And that was the way the conversation ended two weeks ago.

Yesterday

"Governor Jacobs's office, how can I help you?" answered Nancy, the governor's secretary.

"Good morning, Nancy. This is Doug Smith. Is the governor handy?" said the caller.

"Just a minute, Mr. Smith. I'll check." Nancy pushed the intercom button. "Governor, I have the district attorney on the line for you," she said.

"Put him through," said Jacobs. "Good morning, DB, how is everything in the district attorney's office today?" he asked as he touched an icon to scramble the call.

Douglas B. Smith was often referred to as DB by his friends and associates.

"Still trying to separate the good guys from the bad, Governor," he said lightheartedly.

"Okay, Doug, we're secure," replied Governor Jacobs.

"Bill, as you know by now, we were able to get to Mankewitz and took care of that situation. Before he decided to take a swim in the ocean, he told us the Feds were still in the dark about our presence here and just wanted Castoro for mob-related reasons. But here is the real reason I called. The guy we sent down to San Antonio to take care of Marshal Shore has come up missing, and Shore is alive and well. We also seem to have lost your communications flunky. It seems he disappeared in the middle of the night," said Smith.

"Damn," said the governor. "Send two men down to stake out Shore's place and instruct them to take him out at the first opportunity. I'll message Borden, and hopefully, he will respond. If you locate him before I do, just sit on him and report back to me."

"You got it, Governor," replied Smith as Jacobs disconnected.

The governor got up from his chair and stood, looking out the floor-to-ceiling window overlooking downtown Austin. "Shit," he simply said.

Current day

Lyman passed Drake's request up the chain of command, left the ball in their court, and thought nothing more about it until eight days later when he heard Mankewitz's body had washed up on the Jersey shoreline. His boss claimed ignorance, saying he just passed the request on up the chain and heard no more. His instincts told him something was terribly wrong, and he was trying to figure out his next move when his uninvited guest showed up. Now he was cruising up I-35 in the early morning approaching New Braunfels on his way to Austin to pop in on Drake and get some answers.

His mind began to wander to thoughts of Brenda. He met her in his junior year at UTSA. She was majoring in English lit of all things. A lover of poetry, Shakespeare, and Molière, she was full of life and brought a smile to any face that came within ten feet of her. He wasn't the jolliest of fellows after witnessing the horrors of Bosnia, and she lifted him up and made him smile in spite of himself. The child of an African American father and a Vietnamese mother, she took the best genes from each of them to make a stunningly beautiful woman. They were hopelessly in love and planning a life together when she pulled out of a Walgreens parking lot and simply did not see the truck coming from the left. Hit directly in the driver's side door, she was killed instantly. He never dated after that, and his work became his life. The tears blurred his vision as he approached San Marcos.

As he was driving through San Marcos, Lyman's phone rang. Pushing the button on the steering column, he answered it, "Hello."

"Lyman, this is Drake Borden. We need to talk." The fear in his voice was palpable.

"Funny you should say that. I got tired of waiting for you to return my calls and am just passing San Marcos headed your way," Lyman replied.

"No, don't go there! Turn around. I'm parked outside your condo." He almost yelled into the phone.

"Okay, just sit tight and calm down. I'll be there in forty-five minutes," Lyman said as he sped across two lanes of traffic to take the next exit.

Lyman killed the headlights and eased against the curb about a half block from his condo. He would walk slowly and cautiously over to the building, scanning the area closely as he went. It was still dark at 4:45 a.m., and he was about fifty yards from the building entrance when he noticed a dark SUV parked across the street. He took out his cell and called Drake's number and saw a phone light go on in a small white Subaru parked two spaces behind the SUV.

"Hello," Drake answered.

"Drake, Lyman here. I want you to listen carefully and do exactly as I say. Do you understand?"

"Yes," Drake replied.

"Okay, turn off the interior light switch, open the door slowly and only enough so you can get out, and quietly get out of the car, leaving the door open. Walk away to the rear behind the car around the building toward the road. Do it now."

Lyman saw the driver's door open, and Drake slid out as instructed and started heading his way. He was about ten feet behind his car when Lyman saw the interior lights go on in the SUV as two men jumped out of the front doors. One of the men hollered at Drake to stop.

"Run!" Lyman yelled as he drew his Glock 17.

Drake was running full out now, and Lyman heard the report and saw the muzzle flashes from the two men. He returned fire, and the two men scrambled behind the front end of Drake's car. Drake was almost to him now, and he screamed "Keep running!" as he continued to lay down cover fire. Then he ran after Drake toward his parked car, and they jumped in as he laid down rubber, racing away.

Sitting in the Night Owl Diner in a booth with two hot cups of coffee between them, they just sat silently for a few minutes. Drake's hands were wrapped around the hot coffee cup to help control the shaking. "I've never been shot at before, Lyman. I didn't go in the service like you did," he said.

"Trust me, Drake. It's not something you get used to," Lyman replied. "Look, how about you go back to the beginning and explain what prompted you to call me with that request?"

They're Here!!

Drake looked around nervously. "You think we really lost them?" he asked.

"Yes, we lost them. So just try to calm down and start from the beginning, okay?" said Lyman.

Drake took a deep breath, trying to regain his composure. "Have you been following the Charles Mankewitz murder trial in the news lately?" he asked.

"Well, since it has pretty much been dominating the news, yes," Lyman replied. "Dr. James T. Emmons disappeared and was presumed dead after incurring huge gambling debts with the mob. He refused to pay them back or even try and was totally arrogant, thinking they wouldn't dare hurt a renowned UT professor. He was obviously wrong. The circumstantial evidence against Mankewitz was so strong the DA decided to go to trial even though the body was never recovered. During the trial, Mankewitz gave up Giovani Castoro as the one who put out the contract. He is currently in jail awaiting trial, and Mankewitz escaped prison time and was put into the witness protection program," Lyman replied.

Drake leaned over the table and lowered his voice. "Yes, that's the way they played it up. But it was all bullshit."

CHAPTER 3

Six months earlier

Dr. James T. Emmons was a geneticist and professor at the University of Texas in Austin. Widowed at thirty-two when his daughter Julie was ten, he was now forty-four and living in a one-bedroom apartment in Round Rock, just north of Austin. He was on a Skype call with his now twenty-two-year-old daughter when the doorbell rang. *That's odd,* he thought. *Don't get many visitors at 8:45 p.m.* He said goodbye to his daughter and went to the door.

Looking through the peephole, he saw two men in suits standing there, and he opened the door. "Good evening, gentlemen," he said.

"Good evening, Professor," said the taller of the two, who seemed to be in charge.

"What can I do for you?"

"I'm Special Agent Tom Lattimer, and this is Special Agent Jim Fredericks with the FBI," Lattimer said as he and Fredericks flashed their credentials. "May we come in?" he continued.

"By all means," replied Emmons as he motioned them in. "Please have a seat on the couch in the living room," he said as he sat on the recliner across from the couch.

"I'll get right to the point, Professor," Lattimer began as he took out a small ziplock bag from his breast pocket. "I have here a cigarette butt, and we need you to extract a DNA sample from it. Because of some unique security concerns, we would like to avoid using the bureau's facilities and personnel for this. I'm afraid I am not at liberty to explain further except to say you would be doing a great service to your country by helping us. We will visit you again in seventy-two hours to obtain the results and get your report. Thank you, and we'll let ourselves out." And with that, they were gone without waiting for an answer.

What the hell just happened? thought Emmons while looking at the ziplock bag in his hand. *I don't know what they expect to find when I run this, and I don't really know who the hell they are. How do I know their credentials were valid or what their motives are? This is scaring the hell out of me,* he thought as he sat there trying to figure out what to do next. "Okay, Jim," he said to himself, "you're going to go to the lab right now and extract the DNA from this cigarette butt and take a look at it. Then you can decide what to do from there."

Four hours later, Dr. Emmons was in the lab applying aniline dye to the chromosomes of the extracted DNA to make them stand out while viewing through the electron microscope. He was observing the chromosomes and waiting for the point in cell division called the metaphase stage of mitosis. At this stage, the strands are condensed and aligned in one plane. When this occurred, the helix ladder came into focus, and his heart started racing. "What the…oh my god," he whispered.

Two hours later, he sat at his desk staring at the report he had just finished.

At 7:00 a.m. that morning, the janitor arrived and found blood on the floor next to the professor's chair and called the Austin Police Department. Dr. Emmons was never seen again.

CHAPTER 4

"What do you mean by that? It can't all be bullshit," said Lyman. "Who the hell could pull off something like that? The media doesn't just print anything given to them. They do research, have sources, verify information, and investigate. And why would anyone want to fabricate such a story? It makes no sense, Drake."

"Listen," replied Drake, "the state attorney general's office in Austin got an anonymous call asking them to investigate the Dallas office of the FBI. Now normally, they would not respond to an anonymous call, but this person claimed to have firsthand knowledge of who killed Professor Emmons and said it was not Mankewitz. Now you know that it was the Dallas office of the FBI that took the Emmons case away from the Austin Police Department, claiming federal jurisdiction, and subsequently arrested Mankewitz. This source claimed the FBI had been infiltrated by some sort of foreign operative and the DA's office needed to investigate. The DA passed this information on up to the governor's office, and he asked me to see what I could find out about Mankewitz. That's when I called you."

Lyman sat there for a few minutes, digesting what he had just heard. "So why did you not answer my calls after Mankewitz floated ashore in Jersey? And why did you come down here and not want me to go to Austin?" Lyman finally responded.

"When I heard about Mankewitz, I got scared," answered Drake. "First Dr. Emmons and now Mankewitz. Was I next? What was I dealing with here? I swore I was being followed and wondered if my apartment, office, and car were all bugged. I became seriously paranoid and started suffering from insomnia, and then decided I needed to come down here to see you. So about eleven p.m. last night, I snuck out of my apartment and quietly drove out of the parking lot to the main road before turning on my lights. After arriving, I sat for a while before finally calling you, and you know the rest," Drake concluded.

"Okay," Lyman started, "let's break this down. Here's what we know right now. Some person or persons abducted and apparently murdered Professor James T. Emmons in his laboratory in Austin, Texas. The FBI claimed jurisdiction in the case for reasons unknown at this time and took it away from the Austin Police. A gentleman by the name of Charles Mankewitz was arrested and tried for Emmons's murder. The FBI convinced the DA that there was enough circumstantial evidence to convict without having the body. Mr. Mankewitz made a plea bargain with the federal prosecutor to give up crime boss Giovani Castoro in exchange for no jail time and relocation under the witness protection program.

"An anonymous source claimed the Dallas office of the FBI had been infiltrated by a foreign entity and claimed to have firsthand evidence that Mankewitz did not kill Dr. Emmons. This source wants the state district attorney to investigate, and the request is bumped up to the governor's office. You call me to arrange a meeting with Mankewitz. I pass the request on up to my superiors, and eight days later, Mankewitz's body washes up on the Jersey shoreline. While I'm pondering that little bit of information, a gentleman visits me at three thirty in the morning with a silenced .45-caliber Sig Sauer in his hand. Then we pass each other on I-35, I do a U-turn, we meet in front of my condo and get shot at by two unknown subjects, and here we are. Did I leave anything out?" Lyman finished.

"That's about it," said Drake.

Lyman just sat there thinking for a minute. "There is something about a conviction with no body being found that bothers me. Exactly what was the overwhelming circumstantial evidence that led to a conviction without a body?" asked Lyman.

"I don't know," replied Drake.

"Does Emmons have any close living relatives we can talk to?" Lyman continued.

"I believe he has a daughter up in Connecticut attending Yale, and I think his father is still living, but I don't know where," said Drake.

"Well, let's find out," said Lyman.

CHAPTER 5

"What is the one thing Randolph Air Force Base, Kelly Field Annex, Lackland Air Force Base, and Fort Sam Houston all have in common? They are all located in San Antonio, Texas. Well, guess what, Drake?" asked Lyman. "Emmons's dad is a retired Air Force master sergeant living right here in San Antonio. With as many military bases as they have here, it seems like a reasonable choice for a place to retire. He's in the book and lives about seven miles from here. Let's go see if we can catch him in."

David Emmons was seventy years old and widowed, living alone in a three-bedroom house in a subdivision in Northeast San Antonio just off Interstate 35. When he answered the door, Lyman was impressed. He stood about five feet, eleven inches, with gray hair cut in a buzz as if he were still in the military. He was wearing shorts and a tank top with good posture and well-toned arms. He seemed to be in great shape for a man his age.

In the background, Lyman could hear Captain Kirk addressing a Klingon warrior on the television. "Good morning, sir. My name is Deputy Marshal Lyman Shore, and this is my partner, Mr. Drake Borden. I wonder if you would mind answering a few questions about your son James," Lyman said.

Emmons eyed both of them over for a second and then said, "Sure, why not. Come in and have a seat while I shut this off. It will continue recording on the DVR anyway." He walked into the living room, picked up the remote, and shut the TV off. "Can I get you two something to drink? Water, beer, wine, whiskey?" he asked.

"No, thank you, sir. We're fine," Lyman answered for both of them as they sat down on the couch.

"Suit yourself," said Emmons as he popped the top off a beer bottle and proceeded to the recliner. "What can I tell you about my Jimmy?" he asked.

"Well, Mr. Emmons, I guess I'd like to know what you think of how the story was covered and whether your son is dead or alive," said Lyman.

"Total horseshit is what I think. My Jimmy was never a gambler. He was a scientist, for Chrissake. Numbers and calculations were his life, and anyone who knows numbers knows the odds are always stacked against you in the casinos. Him being in debt to the mob was a bunch of crap. Someone has an underlying agenda here, and my boy is still alive somewhere," Emmons replied.

"Did the police or the FBI ever contact you?" Lyman asked.

"No, just those stupid reporters asking their stupid questions about what kind of boy he was and if he got along with other kids and if he had a gambling problem early in life, blah, blah, blah. At first, I tried to tell them the truth, that he was a good student who never got into any trouble and never gambled. But it didn't matter what I said. They wanted to sell papers and get high TV ratings, and 'good boy' stories don't do that," Emmons concluded.

"Thank you, Mr. Emmons. I give you my word that I am going to do everything I can to get to the bottom of this and hopefully find your son alive somewhere. Oh, and one more thing, do you happen to have the phone number for his daughter Julie?" Lyman asked.

"No, but I have her Skype ID," he said as he wrote it down and handed the paper to Lyman.

"Please give me a call if you think of anything else or just want to check on our progress," Lyman said as he stood and handed Emmons a business card.

"Will do, Marshal. Now go find my boy," said Emmons as he opened the front door and gestured them out.

They're Here!!

As they were getting into the car, Lyman told Drake, "We need to Skype Julie and see what she thinks about her father's death. We'll head over to my office in Alamo Heights to make the call. That's a pretty busy area, and I don't think those guys will come after us there," he said.

Alamo Heights was an upscale section of San Antonio not far from downtown, the Alamo and the River Walk. It was where the so-called old money lived.

A pretty young woman with her hair in a ponytail appeared on the screen as Julie answered the Skype call. "Hello," she said.

"Hello, Ms. Emmons. My name is Deputy Marshal Lyman Shore with the US Marshals Service," said Lyman as he showed his credentials to the camera. "I'm looking into the disappearance of your father and wonder if you would mind answering a few questions," he continued.

"I thought they already decided that he was murdered," she said. "They even convicted somebody of the crime."

"Yes, I know," Lyman replied. "But I have my doubts and am conducting an independent investigation into the matter. I would like to get your opinion on the whole thing."

"I think the whole thing was ridiculous," she replied. "Anyone who knew—I mean knows—my father knows he was not a gambler and was not involved with the mob. I guess it made for a great story, so the media just ate it up. I tried to keep telling anyone and everyone who would listen that my dad was still alive, but no one wanted to hear that," she said.

"Can you think of anyone who would benefit from kidnapping him and staging his murder?" asked Lyman.

No, but I was on a Skype call with him the night he disappeared, and he had to go because someone was at the door. That was about 8:30 p.m. It was the next morning they found the blood near his chair at the lab. As far as anyone knows, I was the last person to talk to him," Julie answered.

"Thank you, Julie. I appreciate your cooperation and assure you I will do everything possible to find out what really happened to your father. I'll be in touch," said Lyman.

"Thank you, Marshal Shore. I hope to hear from you soon," said Julie as she ended the call.

"Okay," said Lyman to Drake, "somebody came to Emmons's home about 8:30 p.m., and the next morning, his blood is found next to his chair at his laboratory and he goes missing and presumed dead. What do you say we just jump into this thing with both feet and go on the offensive? I don't appreciate whoever these assholes are who are trying to kill me and then shooting up my neighborhood. Let's just find out who the fuck they are and, while we're at it, where the good doctor is. There are ninety-four US Marshals and almost four thousand deputy US Marshals and criminal investigators in the United States Marshals Service. I am going to harness as many of those resources as I can, and we're going to kick ass and take names. You're sticking with me until we get this thing figured out. Call your boss and tell him you're taking leave for a while because of a family emergency. Right now, I'm going to call the associate director for operations, Phillip Harris, and tell him everything we know up to this point. Well, everything except maybe the part about the guy I killed and threw into an incinerator. I wouldn't want my old Army buddy to have to explain that."

* * * * *

"We have an appointment with the director for 2:30 p.m. tomorrow at his office in Arlington," said Lyman to Drake as he hung up the phone. I don't think it's a good idea to return to my condo just yet, so we'll go shopping for some fresh clothes and spend the night at an airport hotel. We're on a 6:00 a.m. flight to Reagan National Airport tomorrow morning."

Chapter 6

"That's quite a story, Lyman," said Director Harris as they sat in his office in Arlington, Virginia. "My first priority is to determine who gave up Mankewitz. The list of people who knew Mankewitz's whereabouts is not that long, and I have people working on that already. I want you to go visit the Dallas office of the FBI and see what you can dig up on that end. We will have your place staked out in San Antonio in case those two clowns who shot at you show up again," Harris concluded.

"Thank you, sir. We're going to take a run up to New Jersey and look in on the medical examiner before visiting the FBI in Dallas. I'll be in touch," Lyman said as he and Drake exited, closing the door behind them.

* * * * *

The bloated body of Charles Mankewitz was lying on the autopsy table at the medical examiner's office in Newark, New Jersey.

"Well, gentlemen, the cause of death in this case is pulmonary embolism caused by a blood clot in one of the arteries in the lung," the doctor said to Deputy Marshal Shore and Drake as they both looked down on Mankewitz.

"So you're saying this man died of natural causes," replied Shore.

"It would appear so," answered the doctor.

"Thanks, Doc," said Lyman as he headed for the exit with Drake in tow.

"So I ask for an audience with Mr. Mankewitz, and eight days later, he conveniently dies of natural causes, falls into the ocean, and ends up washing ashore in Jersey," says Lyman to Drake as they step outside and head for the car. "Does that sound like a logical sequence of events to you?" asked Lyman rhetorically.

CHAPTER 7

1942

The world was at war—a time of turmoil, death, and destruction as Earth had never seen before. At 2:00 a.m. on October 10, 1942, a huge craft hovered ten thousand feet over the South Pole. It was easily the size of two aircraft carriers, only perfectly round with numerous circular ports throughout the bottom. One of these ports opened, and out shot a smaller vessel of the same shape and design. It rocketed straight into the icy waters. This was all done in virtual silence, and the ships possessed cloaking technology that made them invisible to radar or any other detection methods available to the people of Earth at the time.

The smaller ship leveled off eight hundred feet under the surface of the ocean and two hundred feet from the bottom and began to transform itself into what appeared to be a solid glass-like enclosure consisting of three levels, with personnel moving about on all three levels doing various tasks. The top level contained video screens with scenes of hundreds of different locations around the world, and in the center was a large command chair occupied by a man in a white uniform. He appeared human with short crew cut-type white hair and a white beard and was clearly in charge.

Once the transformation was completed, the ship seemed to just slowly disappear as the ocean reclaimed the area. Then the mother ship shot into space, disappearing from sight in seconds. This was the beginning stage of a plan to make Earth suitable for their kind. Unfortunately, Earth would not be suitable for the current inhabitants when the mission was completed.

In 1943, the commander of the alien ship watched as German U-boats would find it by accident when they bumped into it, stopping their forward motion. They maneuvered all around it, determining its size, but never actually saw anything, much less figure out how to get inside of it. A German admiral would send a message to Hitler, saying he found an impregnable fortress while conveniently leaving out the part about not being able to get inside.

Chapter 8

Giovani Castoro was a second-generation alien. His father, Lorenzo Castoro, assumed the identification of an Italian migrant when he came to Earth years earlier. He was of the soldier class of alien assigned to the area in Austin, Texas, and succeeded in infiltrating the Austin Police Department, going to the academy and then to patrol. Working his way up to lieutenant, he was put in charge of a task force looking into the activities of organized crime in the Austin area. During this time, he made numerous contacts within the major crime families and secured his son, Giovani, employment within one of the families while he was only a teenager. Giovani soon gained favor with Godfather Matteo Ricci and rose through the ranks to lieutenant by the time he was twenty-three. He ascended to godfather status at thirty-eight when he saw his opportunity and put a bullet into Ricci's head, blaming it on a rival family and starting a war that would end with Castoro as the dominant crime boss in the state of Texas.

He was not actively involved with the mission to prepare Earth for the invasion until Command contacted him to fund the construction of factories in Myanmar, Brazil, North Korea, and other countries. Funneling money from prostitution, gambling, and drugs to accounts in those countries had been ongoing for a little over a year before the FBI burst into his office and arrested him on some trumped-up charges of killing some geneticist he knew nothing about. When he was taken somewhere to be interrogated about the invasion, he knew the Mankewitz story was all a clever ruse so they could question him and test his DNA. Somehow, they knew, or at least suspected, he was an alien. Now he didn't know where he was, and he was being interrogated mercilessly day after day. Isolated and subjected to this questioning constantly, he didn't know how long he could hold out. He just wanted them to leave him alone. He could deal with solitary confinement, but this constant grilling was becoming intolerable. It seemed certain that he would be here until his people achieved their objective and freed him, and Earth would finally be a more compatible place for him to live.

Chapter 9

Agents Lattimer and Fredericks stood just inside the doorway of the hangar across the field from the main terminal and one hangar down from the fixed-base operator's office at Dallas Love Field. The hangar was well lit and laid out in two partitioned sections. The first section had a large digital map of the United States on one wall with numerous tags on various locations and about twenty desks facing the display with agents on laptops working. The second section was split into two halves with several desks populated by FBI agents of various forensic specialties and their necessary equipment in one half and a door leading to the other half where more equipment was set up to extract, isolate, and process DNA samples.

Agents Lattimer and Fredericks entered through this door, and seated at a desk looking over some documents was Professor James T. Emmons. The FBI agents walked over to Emmons and sat down in two fold-up chairs in front of the desk.

"The last sample was normal, gentlemen," Emmons said.

"Good," said Lattimer. "We'll brief him and get him in the loop tomorrow morning."

"Tom," said Emmons, "I know how important it is to screen these people before bringing them in, and I fully understand the gravity of the situation we're faced with. But it's been six months now since I disappeared, and it's so unfair for my daughter to have to go through this. I'm just not sure how much more of this I can stand."

Tom Lattimer sat silent for a moment, studying Emmons. "I hear what you're saying, Jim, and I can't tell you how much I appreciate the sacrifice you've made." He paused and looked over at Fredericks for a second and then said, "I'll tell you what I'll do. I'll personally give Julie a visit and break the news to her that her father is alive. She is sure to be ecstatic but furious that we let her think you were dead all this time. So I'll take the brunt of the furious part and do my best to explain the necessity of making everyone believe you were dead without giving any specifics. Then we will give her a couple of days to absorb all this before arranging for you guys to get some quality time together for dinner and wine in a secure location. That way, maybe you'll get mostly hugs and kisses with just a little leftover anger. It will be necessary to impress upon her in the strongest possible terms the need to continue the charade of your death. But she's an intelligent woman, and I'm willing to take the risk if it will keep you here working with us."

Emmons lit up and welled up with joy. "That would be great, Tom. Thank you."

Dr. Emmons wasn't always Dr. Emmons. He was what they used to call a military brat. His father, David R. Emmons, was a noncommissioned officer in the United States Air Force, and little Jimmy was yanked out of school every few years when his daddy would be transferred. He would have to make new friends in a new place and sometimes in a new country. This made him reluctant to have any close friends because he didn't want to have to deal with the pain of leaving them when his daddy transferred again. When he was born, his father was a big fan of the '60s TV show *Star Trek* and named him James Tiberius Emmons after Captain James Tiberius Kirk in the show.

Not wanting to have any close friends and being an only child, he tended to be introverted and focused on his studies and reading to keep his mind occupied. His favorite TV show growing up was *Columbo*. He was fascinated at how Columbo would figure out who committed the crime and wanted to be like Columbo when he grew up. Then when he was fourteen, he read about forensic scientists using blood analysis to identify families of kidnapped children in Argentina and, shortly after that, of DNA fingerprinting, and he decided he wanted to be a geneticist. He was accepted at the Massachusetts Institute of Technology (MIT) with a full four-year scholarship and graduated fourth in his class.

Romance did not come easy for James. He was shy among girls and intimidated by the pretty ones. But in his sophomore year at MIT, Cheryl Babbs sat next to him in the library one day and started talking to him. She was gorgeous, and at first, he didn't understand why she was being so friendly toward him. But she was patient and slowly brought him out of his shell, and soon they were inseparable. He became a whole new person with her and found happiness he never knew existed. Consequently, his studies started to suffer a little, but again, she would keep him focused and encourage him to study hard. He often said he would have been first in his class were it not for being distracted by his love for her. But that was a sacrifice he happily made, for life without her now was unthinkable.

After graduation, they were married and nine months later, their daughter Julie arrived. James went on to the University of Michigan to obtain his doctorate in genetics prior to accepting a teaching position at the University of Texas at Austin. Two years later, he opened a private DNA testing facility in that city. Cheryl was a stay-at-home mom until the DNA testing facility opened, after which she managed the financial side of that business. Their life could not have been better at that time. The three of them would go on family outings on weekends—river rafting, water parking, or maybe to an air show at Bergstrom Air Force Base.

Then when Julie was ten, their world was savagely attacked by the life-eating creature called cancer. Following a routine mammogram and a biopsy, Cheryl was diagnosed with stage III invasive breast cancer. Months of chemotherapy was followed by radiation treatments and then the inevitable and unthinkable. Cheryl was gone, and James would have jumped in the grave with her if he didn't have a daughter to care for. So he carried on with his life and focused his attention on Julie. She graduated high school with straight As and was accepted at Yale, where she was currently in her senior year majoring in political science. When she went away to Connecticut, James sold the house in Austin and moved into a one-bedroom condo in Round Rock. He stayed in close contact with Julie through Skype, Messenger, and email. They were on a Skype call when the two FBI agents rang the doorbell.

CHAPTER 10

American Airlines Flight 227 from Newark, New Jersey, to Dallas/Fort Worth International Airport arrived on time, and Lyman Shore and Drake Borden picked up the rental car and headed for the Dallas office of the FBI.

Malcolm Ferguson was an African American who grew up poor in rural Georgia and bucked the odds by getting a degree in finance from Georgia Tech and a scholarship to Harvard Law. Now forty-four years old, he stood six foot three and was the special agent in charge of the Dallas office of the FBI. As he sat behind his desk, his secretary Amanda Boudria's voice came over the phone speaker.

"Sir, there is a gentleman from the Marshals office here to speak with you," she said.

Ferguson pushed the button on the intercom and replied, "Send him in, Amanda."

The door opened, and Lyman came in, with Drake following behind. "I appreciate you taking the time to see us, Special Agent Ferguson. This is my colleague Drake Borden, communications director from the governor's office," said Lyman.

"Nice to meet you. What can I do for you, gentlemen?" asked Ferguson, getting right to the point.

Lyman went through the history of events leading up to his visit, concluding with, "So, Special Agent Ferguson, can you shed any light on why the FBI claimed jurisdiction over the Emmons case, who the anonymous source may have been who claimed your office had been influenced by a foreign entity, and why they may have claimed Mankewitz was innocent in the death of Emmons?"

Ferguson silently studied the two men for a minute and then said, "Would you two have any objection to submitting to a DNA test?" He saw the confused look on both of their faces and continued, "It's not negotiable if you would like to pursue this matter further."

Lyman looked at Drake and then back at Ferguson and said, "Sure, no problem. Swab away."

Ferguson swabbed the inside of each of their cheeks and placed the swab sticks in individual tubes and marked them. "Leave your number with Amanda, and we will contact you in a day or two. I believe you can find your way out," he said as he sat back down behind his desk and began tapping on his laptop keyboard. As the door closed behind Lyman and Drake, Ferguson picked up his cell. "Lattimer? We need to talk," he said.

Lyman and Drake found a mom-and-pop restaurant to have dinner and checked in at the local Holiday Inn for the night. The national news was all about global warming and how scientists were trying to figure out why there seemed to be further ozone depletion after years of stabilization following the Montreal Protocol.

"The Montreal Protocol is an international treaty adopted in Montreal on September 16, 1987, that attempted to regulate the production and use of chemicals that contribute to the depletion of Earth's ozone layer," the talking head on the television explained. "The treaty has nearly two hundred signatories and went into effect on January 1, 1989."

Around midnight, Lyman went to bed but found himself just lying there with the usual visions haunting him. The mass graves he had seen while driving around the Baltics in his tank were bad enough, but the picture of one particular little girl, perhaps five or six, all dressed up in a pretty dress lying there in the mass grave, eyes open, with a stuffed bear next to her was burned into his brain forever. How Mother Teresa and the monsters who did that could be creatures of the same species was beyond his comprehension. He didn't know what time he finally drifted off but was awakened by Drake knocking on his door about 7:30 a.m.

"Jesus," said Drake as Lyman opened the door. "Did you sleep in those clothes? You look like hell."

"Have a seat," replied Lyman. "I'm gonna jump in the shower and work on getting my appearance up to your standards."

Twenty minutes later, he reappeared dressed in clean clothes with hair combed and face clean-shaven. "Am I pretty enough to be seen in public with you now, sweetheart? Come on, asshole. I'll buy you breakfast," he said as he headed for the door.

About forty-five minutes later, as Lyman and Drake finished their coffee, Lyman's cell rang. "Hello," he said.

"Lyman, this is Director Harris. I've got some good news and some bad news for you. How do you want it?" asked Harris.

"Give me the good news first," Lyman replied.

"Okay, well, the good news is, your two buddies showed up at your condo again. The bad news is, they decided to go down shooting and are both dead, so we won't be getting any information out of them. Neither of them had any ID, so we'll be taking prints, DNA, etc. to see if we can determine who the hell they are. I'll keep you posted."

Lyman told him about his meeting with Ferguson, and they agreed to keep each other informed as to their progress.

Lyman paid the check and was getting in the rental car when the phone went off again. "Hello," he said.

"Deputy Marshal Shore? This is Special Agent Ferguson. You have time to take a ride?" Ferguson asked.

"I suppose so. Where to?" Lyman replied.

"Meet me at White Rock Lake Park in one hour. And make sure you're not followed," said Ferguson.

Forty-five minutes later, Lyman and Drake were parked at the entrance to White Rock Lake Park, waiting for Ferguson. He arrived ten minutes later in a dark-blue Chevy Tahoe.

"Get in guys," he said out the window as he pulled alongside.

Lyman took the shotgun position, and Drake jumped in the back.

"Where to now, boss?" asked Lyman.

"You'll know soon enough. The reason I had you meet me out here is so I could pick up any tails between the office and here. I will give you credit for making sure you weren't followed either," Ferguson answered.

"A bit cloak and dagger, all this, don't you think, Special Agent?" Lyman asked.

"You will understand the need for it shortly, Deputy Marshal," Ferguson retorted.

A short time later, they were at Dallas Love Field on the other side of the field from the main passenger terminal. As they passed by a large hangar and the fixed-base operations building, Lyman noticed another smaller hangar come into view, and the Tahoe pulled around to the field side and parked near a door marked Authorized Personnel Only. Surveillance cameras could be seen at various locations.

"Here we are, gentlemen. Follow me, please," Ferguson said as he got out of the vehicle and walked to the door. He punched in a six-digit combination, and a click was heard as he opened the door to the hangar. Lyman and Drake followed him in and didn't know what to make of what they were looking at.

Agents Lattimer and Fredericks approached, with Lattimer offering his hand to Lyman. "Welcome to my world, Deputy Marshal Shore," he said. "I think we have a lot of explaining to do, so follow me, and we'll get started," he continued as he walked further into the hangar.

Lyman and Drake followed Lattimer and Fredericks with Ferguson taking up the rear. They went past the large digital map of the US, through the next section, and into the DNA laboratory where a gentleman was seated, staring into an electron microscope.

Lattimer walked over to the man and turned back to Lyman. "Deputy Shore, Mr. Borden, I'd like you to meet Professor James T. Emmons, a true patriot and very much alive," he said with a big smile on his face.

CHAPTER 11

Lyman stood there with a hundred questions rolling around in his brain. He was very pleased but not surprised to find Emmons alive and thought to himself, *There better be a good reason why Emmons's father and daughter weren't told and spared the grief of thinking he may be dead.* Drake was stunned and speechless.

Lattimer continued, "I know you have a lot of questions, but I think it best that I give you some background information first. How much do you know about global warming, Deputy?"

"Well, just that it has something to do with the depletion of the ozone layer and not everyone believes in it," replied Lyman.

"Actually," said Lattimer, "ozone depletion happens when chlorofluorocarbons are released into the stratosphere and the chlorine and bromine interact with ozone molecules, changing them to ordinary oxygen molecules, which can no longer absorb the harmful UV-B rays coming from the sun. Global warming occurs when carbon dioxide [CO_2] and other air pollutants collect in the atmosphere and absorb sunlight and solar radiation that have bounced off Earth's surface. Normally, this radiation would escape into space, but these pollutants, which can last for years to centuries in the atmosphere, trap the heat and cause the planet to get hotter. That's what's known as the greenhouse effect. Some folks may not want to believe it, but these are scientifically proven facts. The one thing these two phenomena have in common is, they both contribute to the destruction of the ozone layer."

Lyman sat down and said, "I assume you're going somewhere with all this?"

"Bear with me, Lyman," continued Lattimer. "Ultraviolet B or UVB rays from the sun can alter DNA, damage the immune system, and cause cancer, blindness, cataracts, and premature aging among other things. Ozone absorbs these rays, preventing them from reaching Earth's surface. If the ozone layer were to disappear completely, all life on Earth would be destroyed in short order. So let me get to the point. After years of stabilization, scientists were seeing ozone depletion occurring again at a rather alarming rate. They began to notice it in early 2015 and set out to find an explanation. More recently, these same scientists have also noted a dramatic increase in the level of carbon dioxide in the atmosphere, which will accelerate global warming.

"A chemist by the name of Andrea Nichols was the first one to bring all this to the attention of the scientific community. She lost her life in a car accident shortly after that. Then other scientists studying this noticed new holes in the ozone in areas other than the North and South Poles. As this information was being uncovered, more untimely deaths occurred, and we were brought in to investigate. While all the deaths were deemed to be of natural causes or accidents, we knew something was not right when scientists with these particular areas of expertise were dying at a rate statistically too high to be just chance.

"We put surveillance on some of the key people who were working on this and caught a man tampering under the hood of one of their cars. When confronted, he ran, and when ordered to stop, he pulled out a gun and started firing at our agents. They returned fire, killing him. He had no ID, and his prints were not in any database, but it was when we ran his DNA that things got really interesting. I'll let Dr. Emmons explain that part of it. Doctor?"

"Good morning, gentlemen," Dr. Emmons began. "When the chemist looked at the DNA helix under the electron microscope, he couldn't believe his eyes. It was not human or from any life-form on this planet. Nuclear DNA in the cell of all human beings is made up of four chemical basis: [A] adenine, [G] guanine, [C] cytosine, and [T] thyronine. The adenine attaches to the guanine, and the cytosine attaches to the thyronine, making the two alternating rungs of the DNA helix. The DNA of this man, or whatever he was, had six chemical basis with [E] ethionine and [U] uracil attached to each other to make a third rung on the helix ladder. This was quite an astonishing discovery, as you can imagine—a life-form not of this planet that looks and acts like any normal human being. And with that, I'll turn it back to Agent Lattimer," Emmons concluded.

"Subsequently, an autopsy was performed, and other anomalies were discovered," Lattimer continued. "The subject was found to be wearing a type of contact lens on both eyes that we had never seen before. Analysis indicated that these lenses intensified the amount of ultraviolet radiation getting through. Also, his blood had high amounts of CO_2, enough to kill a normal human being. In addition to this, his lungs appeared to be under stress. It would appear that the air these creatures would be used to breathing would have to contain a higher level of carbon dioxide and less oxygen than we humans breathe. Consequently, breathing our air takes a toll on their lungs. As we continued our investigation, the unusual ozone depletion continued and people investigating the probable cause continued to die or disappear at an alarming rate in spite of our best efforts to protect them. That is when we realized we must have been infiltrated. We had no idea how many of these things were among us, who they were, or what positions of power and authority they may hold. Since we no longer knew who we could trust inside the bureau, we went outside the loop and recruited Dr. Emmons.

"By this time, we had exposed and killed several others who were stalking some of our scientists. Although given the opportunity to surrender, all decided to resist and had to be killed. All of them were without ID, not in any database, and had the same six-base DNA, contact lenses, etc. as the first subject. Agent Fredericks and I brought Dr. Emmons a DNA sample from one of them, and when he reported it to be a six-base helix, we knew he could be trusted, so we persuaded him to join us in screening agents before adding them to the task force we created to try to get to the bottom of this.

"We refer to these aliens as ALF [alien life-form] and believe they are behind the recent increase in ozone depletion as well as an increase in pollutants in the atmosphere, contributing to global warming. These creatures appear to come from a world with much less ozone protection and may be attempting to duplicate that environment here on planet Earth. If they succeed in destroying enough of the ozone layer and at the same time accelerate the rate of global warming, then we are looking at no less than the destruction of the world as we know it. We don't know where they came from or how they got here and can only guess at their ultimate goal. We also don't know their numbers or command structure or how widespread they are. Are they just in the US, or do they have people throughout the globe? We just don't know at this time," Lattimer finished and waited for Lyman's response.

"So how did Mankewitz fit in to all this?" Lyman asked.

"Mankewitz came into our office looking like the shit had been scared out of him. He claimed to have heard a phone conversation his boss, Giovani Castoro, was having with an unknown person and was afraid if Castoro found out, he would have him killed. He was hesitant to tell us what the conversation was about, but when pressed, he claimed Castoro was talking to someone about destroying something called the ozone layer. He said he had enough information on Mr. Castoro regarding his criminal activities to put him away for a long time and would testify in exchange for being placed into the witness protection program. Coincidentally, Castoro had been a person of interest to us regarding the ALF case. We had uncovered evidence that he had been financing the construction of factories in North Korea, Myanmar, Somalia, and Nicaragua and suspected that he may be an ALF.

"We were working on getting a warrant when Mankewitz showed up. We needed to catch one of these things alive to interrogate, so we devised the charade of Emmons's murder, planted evidence to implicate Mankewitz, and busted in and arrested Castoro after reaching a fabricated plea deal with Mankewitz. But Castoro was not taken to jail but to a secret location for interrogation and put on twenty-four-hour suicide watch. His DNA was taken and did in fact verify him to be an ALF. We have been questioning him for nearly three months now but have not been able to get much out of him. We believe the anonymous call to the governor's office was made by an ALF in order to discredit the FBI and stir things up in an effort to locate Mankewitz.

"It must have worked somewhat because when you passed the request on up the ladder to talk to Mankewitz, a sequence of events occurred that allowed them to find him and kill him. Once that was done, they decided to clean up loose ends and kill you and probably Drake and maybe even the governor. We've got extra eyes on the governor just in case. We feel certain they would have interrogated Mankewitz before killing him so they may know Castoro is not in jail but under interrogation and will double their efforts to find and silence him also," Lattimer concluded.

Lyman sat in silence for a moment, taking all this in. "The two men who shot at us in the parking lot of my condo have been shot and killed by federal marshals," he finally said.

"I'll see if I can get the bodies brought here."

"Good idea," replied Lattimer. "But you can't tell your boss or anyone else what I've told you until their DNA has been tested," he finished.

"Understood," said Lyman as he turned to Emmons. "Professor Emmons, glad to see you're okay, and thanks for all you have done and are continuing to do. I've spoken to your father and daughter, neither of whom believed you were dead. Hopefully, we will be able to tell them the truth before too long."

"Thank you, Marshal, I hope so," replied Emmons.

"Okay, Special Agent Ferguson, if you will be so kind as to take us back to my car, then we'll get out of your hair for a while. I'm gonna see if I can round up a couple of probable ALF corpses and get them down here for Dr. Emmons to examine," Lyman said as he headed for the door.

CHAPTER 12

Orion Dorlestor was the ALF high commander for Earth operations. From the Command and Control Center located eight hundred feet below the Antarctic ice shelf, he controlled and coordinated all Earth operations. He is on a video call with the governor of Texas.

"Governor, your insistence in going after Mr. Mankewitz is causing more problems than it solved. Now we have the US Marshals Service to deal with in addition to the FBI. This man Shore is running around asking questions and stirring up the pot, and I've lost more soldiers in the last week than the previous year. I want Shore and your flunky Drake gone and this hole plugged up. Do you hear me?"

"Yes, Commander, I hear you," replied Jacobs. "But there is no way anyone could have foreseen this deputy marshal being such a problem."

"Just take care of it and do it quickly," said Dorlestor and terminated the call.

Chapter 13

Lyman Shore and Drake Borden were in seats 25E and 25F when their Southwest Airlines flight lifted off from Dallas Love Field en route to San Antonio.

"Well, Drake," he began, "it looks like you're stuck with me for the foreseeable future, my friend. We seem to be on top of the ALF hit list, so I think it best that we stick together."

Drake was squirming around like he had a load in his pants. "You don't really buy into all that crap about aliens among us and such, do you?"

"Sure," replied Lyman. "I mean, who could make up shit like that? And DNA don't lie, buddy. Look, Drake, we're gonna take this one baby step at a time, watch our ass, and let it all sink in. Right now, we focus on getting those two bodies shipped to the FBI in Dallas, if it's not too late."

When they touched down and were taxiing to the gate in San Antonio, no sooner had Lyman turned his cell back on than it was ringing. He looked at the caller ID. "Shit, I think it's too late. Hello, Director Harris. We just landed in San Antonio and are taxiing to the gate as we speak," he said.

Director Harris was not one to be easily disturbed, but his tone told Lyman this was one of those times. "Lyman, I'm here in San Antonio, and I need you to get down to your office ASAP. We need to talk."

"Yes, sir, but I wanted to arrange for the two bodies of my visitors to be sent to the FBI in Dallas for study first," Lyman replied.

Harris raised his voice. "Lyman, the autopsies have been done and DNA taken and processed. Now get the hell down to your office. I'll meet you there in thirty minutes," he said and hung up.

"Well, shit" Lyman said to Drake as they deplaned. "We're going to my office to meet Harris. The bodies have already been processed."

Drake looked like he was on the verge of a nervous breakdown as he stated, "What the hell is happening, Lyman? The world's gone crazy." He was shaking his head back and forth as they walked down the concourse to the lower-level parking garage.

Arriving at the office, Lyman unlocked the door and entered with Drake and Harris right behind.

Harris closed the door and said, "Deputy Marshal Shore, if there is something you're not telling me, I suggest you tell me now."

Shore stared at Harris briefly and then said, "With all due respect, sir, you first."

Harris stared at Shore as his face turned slightly red, and Lyman could see a vein throbbing on his forehead. "Okay," Harris began, "let me just start with this. It turns out those two goons who shot at you are not from this planet. At least that's what their DNA is telling us. But why is it I get the feeling you already knew that?"

Lyman sat down behind the desk and motioned Harris and Drake to take a seat in front. "I suspected it, but only after a lengthy FBI briefing Mr. Borden and I had yesterday." Lyman felt Harris would not have divulged the DNA information if he were an ALF and agreed to tell him everything if he would agree to have his DNA taken and tested following the briefing to remove all doubt. Once the whole story was told, Lyman finished with, "After your DNA comes back clean, we can arrange for you and Ferguson to meet and figure out how the Marshals Service and the FBI can best work together on this. And I would like to suggest that someone reach out to INTERPOL. We don't know how far-reaching this is. One more thing, sir, if and when you figure out who the leak is who gave up Mankewitz, I would suggest you don't arrest him or alert him but put a tail on him. We only have one of them in custody being questioned, and he is not giving much up. These people tend to go down in a blaze of glory rather than surrender when confronted. I'm going back to Dallas to see what else I can get out of Special Agent in Charge Ferguson and brief him on what transpired here today."

Then he and Drake walked out the door, jumped into the Camaro, and headed for the airport to catch a flight back to Love Field.

CHAPTER 14

Arriving in the baggage claim area at Love Field, Lyman felt uneasy. He just had a sense they were being watched. It's a sixth sense that some people in law enforcement seem to develop over time. He looked around and saw nothing unusual or anyone paying too much attention to them, so he shrugged it off. "Don't go and get all paranoid now, Lyman. Maintain your cool," he told himself as they proceeded outside to wait for the shuttle to the car rental location.

It was a busy place, with cars pulling over just long enough to pick up arriving passengers and popping trunks open as they stopped to load the baggage. A police officer was keeping the traffic moving. They crossed the road onto the island to wait for the rental bus on the next lane. Lyman made a mental note of a car that came through without pulling in to pick anyone up. It had a single male driver in it, and Lyman made eye contact with him as he drove by. *Either the person he's picking up is not out yet or he's not here to pick anyone up,* he thought.

When the bus arrived, Lyman put Drake in front of him and told him to sit in the last row against the back window. He wanted to have a clear view of the fifteen or so other passengers on the bus and not have to worry about anyone behind him. They drove away from the terminal and turned left toward the rental offices. Then Lyman looked out the left window and saw the same car he had seen at the terminal pass the bus, and no one was in the passenger's seat. As they pulled up to the building, he saw the car parked in front with no one inside. He scanned the area around the bus but did not see the man he had seen in the car earlier. "Okay, so if I were sent out here to kill us, what would I do?" Lyman asked himself. "I would find a spot where I could see everyone coming from the rental desk to the garage where the cars are and pick us off in the garage while we were trying to find our car," he decided.

"Drake, I want you to find the men's room and lock yourself in one of the stalls until I come for you. If I don't come for you in the next twenty minutes, grab the first taxi you can get and go directly to the FBI office in Dallas and have them get Director Phillip Harris of the US Marshals office on the phone for you and tell him what happened. I'm guessing there is an ALF hit man here waiting for us to enter that rental garage to take us out. I'm going to try to find him first. You understand?" Lyman asked.

"Yes, but why don't we both just grab a taxi now?" he asked.

"Because that's just not the way it works. I don't like it when people try to kill me and my friends. So go find the men's room," said Lyman as he pushed Drake toward the door.

Lyman went inside and signed the rental agreement at the desk and picked up his key, but then instead of walking to the garage, he took the elevator up two levels. He was guessing that the gunman would have gone one level up and taken a position where he was looking down on the renters as they entered the garage. As he exited the elevator, he turned to the right and looked down between the railings to the floor below to the area he thought the ALF would be set up, and sure enough, he saw the man crouched in front of a parked car with a scoped rifle resting on the railing and aimed just where he thought it would be. Now that he knew where the gunman was, he took the elevator back down one level and circled around behind him. With the ALF between the parked car and the railing, he couldn't get a clear shot with his 9 mm Glock, so he waited.

A few minutes later, he saw the barrel come off the railing and knew he was dismantling the rifle and placing it back in his pack. As he got up and started walking around the car, Lyman leveled the 9 mm at him and said, "Freeze, US Marshal. Put your hands on top of your head, interlocking your fingers, and get down on your knees, *now*!" The man stopped and put his hands on his head. "On your knees," Lyman repeated. The man then turned and ran to the guardrail and jumped over it, falling to the concrete floor below. Lyman ran after him and looked down at his broken body below. "Son of a bitch," he said, shaking his head.

After collecting Drake from the stall in the men's room, Lyman called Director Harris and updated him on recent events. "I left the mess for the locals to figure out," he told Harris. "I figure we've got enough ALF bodies to dissect for the time being, and I didn't want to get bogged down trying to explain all this shit to the DPD. Suffice it to say that these guys have not given up on killing us. But what I don't understand is how they knew we would be flying into Love Field when we did."

"Good question," said Harris. "Glad you guys are safe. Good work, Deputy."

"Thanks," replied Lyman and ended the call. Lyman stood thinking and then said to Drake, "Deputy Harris was the only one who knew we were flying to Love Field."

"Well, he and the governor," said Drake.

"What!" said Lyman.

"The governor sent me a text asking how I was and when I was coming back to work. I mentioned I was on my way to Love Field to take care of some things."

"Holy shit. Any further communications with the governor goes through me from now on, got it?" Lyman said.

"Yes, but you don't think—"

"Don't ask," interrupted Lyman.

Chapter 15

The attorney general of the United States, Kenneth Zimmerman, walked into his office where FBI director James Kalahar was waiting. "Good morning, Jim," he said.

Zimmerman was six-two and, at sixty-six years old, was carrying a respectful stomach and a red nose, the product of a lifelong love affair with good whiskey. As a young ALF in his early twenties, he discovered that, in his particular case, alcohol seemed to ease the pain of breathing in too much oxygen. He was strategically placed in an orphanage as a child to be adopted by an affluent couple in New England who were unable to have children. A Harvard Law School graduate, he was hired by a prestigious Boston law firm and went on to become a prominent appellate court judge. As a teenager, he was approached by the ALF in charge of the Boston area and told who he was and given his mission. Following a difficult period of anger and denial, he was properly indoctrinated and eventually came to understand and accept his responsibility to his people. He made the right connections and paved his way to where he was today.

"Good morning, Ken," replied Kalahar.

"Let's get started, shall we?" said Zimmerman.

They discussed ongoing FBI investigations and other matters related to law enforcement.

"Can you tell me what's going on down in Dallas with Ferguson and his team?" Zimmerman asked with somewhat of an angry tone.

"Well, sir, there seems to be growing concern with the public and in the media with the issue of ozone depletion and global warming. Ferguson has identified a number of suspicious deaths involving scientists and others working on this problem and asked me if he could set up an 'under the radar' task force to look into it. I told him to go ahead and gave him 120 days to wrap this up."

Zimmerman's face reddened as he bellowed out, "I'm not concerned with fake news about the damn ozone and global warming! It's just a bunch of Liberals and Democrats making shit up to get attention. Tell Ferguson to shut this task force down immediately and move on to other more important matters."

Kalahar just nodded okay as he left, closing the door behind him. Kalahar had no intention of telling Ferguson to shut down the task force. If anything, he would have him accelerate efforts to find these bastards and stop this insanity. Zimmerman tipped his hand and did what he and Ferguson expected he would. *Great,* thought Kalahar, *the highest law enforcement official in the country is an ALF. Shit, shit, shit!*

CHAPTER 16

James Kalahar was also from New England, growing up in a middle-class family in South Boston, known as South B. He was a tough kid in a tough neighborhood and grew up street-smart. His dad was a fireman and his mom a middle school teacher, and he had two younger sisters that he was very protective of. After graduating from South Boston High School, he went on to get an associate's degree in criminal justice from Bristol Community College in Fall River, Massachusetts, and married his high school sweetheart. Coming from a family with a history of military service, he felt obligated to do his part to serve his country and enlisted in the Army when he was twenty-one. After three years in the Signal Corps, he was honorably discharged and went back to school under the GI Bill. He obtained a bachelor's degree in business administration from Boston College and went on to Boston Law School where he graduated third in his class. He worked for a private detective agency doing surveillance on cheating husbands and such to support his family while going to school. His wife worked as a waitress at a local restaurant while they somehow managed to raise a son and daughter. After graduating from Boston Law School, he went to the Boston Police Academy and began a career in law enforcement, taking him twenty years later to where he was today as director of the Federal Bureau of Investigation.

No sooner was Kalahar out the door than Zimmerman was on a secure line making a call.

"Good morning, Commander. Ferguson will be closing down the task force shortly, so don't worry. Look, we have to do something to get the media's attention off ozone depletion. I'm going to send one of our soldiers out to create a diversion and get their attention off environmental matters for a while. We may have to accelerate the time line. We need 60 percent depletion of the ozone before enough of the assholes on this planet die off to allow us to start bringing our people in. Our sun will run out of fuel in less than fifty years. I'll instruct the soldier to do whatever it takes to get the media talking about something else and to do it quickly. I'm not going to ask for the details, but I expect to hear the networks talking about something unrelated to global warming or ozone depletion very soon," finished Zimmerman as he hung up the phone.

Two days later, Jacob Sutherland woke up with a mission. Today would be his last day to live, and he was okay with that. His home planet, Veteris Orbis, was in the last stages of its life, with temperatures dropping lower every day as the sun began its slow agonizing downward spiral before completely running out of fuel. He would be a martyr for his people today. Wearing a suicide belt packed with explosives under his jacket, he calmly mingled with a huge crowd gathered in Central Park, Manhattan, for a concert to benefit recent hurricane victims. Shortly after the concert began and with music blaring over the crowd, he detonated. The carnage was unfathomable, with hundreds killed and wounded. This story would dominate the world headlines for weeks to come and keep the FBI busy investigating the how and why of it. Attorney General Zimmerman could not have been happier.

Chapter 17

Antoine Laurent was the secretary general of the International Criminal Police Organization, better known as INTERPOL, in Lyon, France. He was sitting at home at 8:30 p.m. when breaking news came on the television about a suicide bomber in New York City's Central Park killing hundreds during a charity concert.

This cannot be as arbitrary and senseless as it would seem, he thought to himself. *Someone has an agenda here, and I hope the NYPD and FBI can figure it out. Prior to this breaking news, the AFP, BBC, Associated Press, and Reuters had all been reporting about increased levels of carbon dioxide in the atmosphere and renewed depletion of the ozone layer. Is it possible this attack in New York could be somehow related to that?* he wondered.

About twelve kilometers from the secretary general lived Thomas Martin with his wife and two teenage sons. They were also watching the news. He and his wife were second-generation ALFs, and the two boys, third. They were saddened not only at the loss of their compatriot who had sacrificed his life for the survival of all the people of their planet but also for the loss of human life. They all felt conflicted by the situation they found themselves in and fervently hoped that maybe a solution would be found that would allow for the survival of everyone. All their friends, neighbors, and coworkers were human. Martin and his family were all wearing masks and hooked up to portable CO_2 tanks to get their carbon dioxide levels back up after breathing the air on Earth all day. It was winter in France, and they had the portable insert in the fireplace that was provided by Command, as did hundreds of other ALF families in Lyon and throughout Europe. As they burned wood in the fireplace, the inserts produced fully halogenated halocarbons that were released through the chimney. All the hydrogen atoms replaced by ozone-killing chlorine with an atmospheric lifetime of one hundred to five hundred years. While they wanted their race to survive, they were hoping another way could be found so their human friends would not have to be sacrificed. There had to be a way, and they considered pulling the inserts from the fireplace.

The soldier element of the invading force was a completely different breed than those sent to enter mainstream society and blend in to assume normal lives. The soldiers were isolated and kept off the grid. No identification or social security numbers or fingerprints on file. Their purpose was to keep the mission moving forward and remove any and all threats to that mission. They did not question orders given to them and would die before allowing capture. They were provided with false "dead end" IDs and cash from Command in order to obtain food, shelter, and other necessities. They were armed with weapons and ammunition purchased anonymously at gun shows in the United States or through the dark web elsewhere. Some of them were embedded within the military of numerous countries, and they were approximately five hundred thousand strong scattered around the globe.

Once the mission was completed, they would comprise the initial contingent of the Global Police Force. There would no longer be individual countries or armies. One central governing council would be created at a location yet to be determined, and society would be set up to duplicate that of the home planet of Veteris Orbis. There would be no religion, and all citizens would have equal rights under their law. The criminal justice system would be based on rehabilitation and reconciliation rather than punishment on the first level. In cases where that failed and in capital cases such as murder, evidence would be collected and guilt or innocence determined. If guilty, death would be the punishment to be carried out within one month with no appeal process. Convicted pedophiles and rapists would be castrated immediately upon conviction. Neither police nor civilians would carry guns, and the dark web would be shut down. Security and the safety of the population would take priority over privacy concerns. No one would be homeless, and no one would go hungry.

Unknown to Thomas Martin, two ALF soldiers were sitting outside his house, monitoring and measuring the chlorine and bromine levels coming out of his chimney. The inserts had a certain capability, and it was their job to make sure the families were meeting their quota. If not, they would receive a visit. Teams such as this were monitoring ALF families throughout Europe. Other teams were watching the factories in other countries to assure continuous emissions of toxins into the stratosphere. All teams reported to and received their instructions from the Command and Control Center under the ice in the Antarctic, who, in turn, received instructions from the High Council of the home planet of Veteris Orbis.

CHAPTER 18

Lyman and Drake were just getting in their rental car when Lyman's phone rang. He looked at the screen, and the name Lattimer appeared. "What's up Tom?" he answered.

"I just got a call from Ferguson, who just got a call from FBI director James Kalahar. It seems Kalahar has borrowed you from the Marshals office and put you under our direction for a while," Lattimer said.

"Okay, just so happens I'm at Love Field about to come see you," replied Lyman.

"Don't bother," said Lattimer. "Part 2 of why I called is because we need you to go to France. Director Harris took you up on your suggestion to call INTERPOL and passed it along to Director Kalahar. He called the international police and spoke with Secretary General Antoine Laurent. The director wants you to go to Lyon and brief him on everything. This thing is big, and we need an international partner. You're booked on American Airlines at 6:20 p.m. for Paris with a connection to Lyon in the morning. You'll be met on arrival by someone from his office. They will be holding up a sign with your name on it in the baggage claim area. Secretary Laurent is bilingual, so you won't need to brush up on your French. We want to determine if they have uncovered any activity that could be tied to our problem here and devise a joint operational plan to head this thing off while we still have a planet," concluded Lattimer.

"Okay, no time to go to San Antonio and pack, so I'll be stopping between here and the DFW Airport to pick up some fresh clothes for the trip. Do I give my receipts to the FBI or the Marshals Service?" asked Lyman.

"Try giving them to the French. Their deficit isn't nearly as big as ours," joked Lattimer.

"One more thing before I go, Tom. I know you have eyes on Governor Jacobs for his protection, but I have reason to believe he is an ALF. Start paying attention to where he goes and who he comes in contact with keeping that in mind. I'll explain in more detail when I get back from France," said Lyman.

"Damn! These guys are everywhere. We'll keep an eye on him, and see you when you get back," said Lattimer before ending the call.

"Well, Drake, it looks like I'm going to France to coordinate all this shit with the head of INTERPOL. We're going shopping for some clothes so I will make a good impression, and then I'll drop you off with the FBI and have Ferguson babysit you while I'm gone."

"Fuck," said Drake uncharacteristically. "I want my life back."

It was cloudy and seventy-two degrees Fahrenheit in Dallas when Lyman boarded his flight and thirty-four degrees Fahrenheit in Lyon when he arrived the next morning at 11:45 a.m. It was January, and Lyman was not accustomed to these temperatures. His hometown of San Antonio rarely saw temperatures below sixty. Secretary Laurent's man was waiting on arrival with the sign as promised, and Lyman hurried into the warmth of the back seat of the car.

Twenty minutes later, they were pulling up to a large government building, and while he was trying to figure out how to open the door, the driver opened it for him. He got out and was escorted by a gorgeous brunette in a tight dress and pumps to the interior elevator. She welcomed him to Lyon in English with a French accent as they ascended to the seventeenth floor, and just for a second, he thought he was falling in love.

As the door opened, a middle-aged man with salt-and-pepper hair dressed in a finely tailored suit greeted him. "Bonjour, monsieur, I am Secretary General Antoine Laurent. Welcome to Lyon," said

Laurent with a French accent that somehow did not have the same impact on Lyman.

"Deputy Marshal Lyman Shore with the United States Marshals Service. A pleasure to meet you, sir," replied Lyman as they vigorously shook hands.

"Follow me, please, Marshal Shore," said Laurent as he led Lyman into a large office with a mahogany desk facing the door and a large window behind it overlooking Lyon. The office was nicely appointed with tasteful paintings of mostly landscapes on the walls, and displayed on the desk were two framed photos of Laurent and who Lyman assumed to be his wife and family. He took his seat behind the desk and motioned Lyman to sit in one of the two chairs facing it.

"So where should we begin?" he asked.

Lyman began slowly going through everything from the beginning while carefully noting Laurent's reactions to what he was saying in an effort to detect any signs that Laurent might be an ALF. By the time he finished, he was fairly certain Laurent was human.

"Marshal Shore, if what you say is true, we must indeed work together to fight this common enemy. I will assemble a team to investigate this immediately, and we will need to teleconference over a secure line at least weekly. I will arrange a meeting with President Dubois to brief him as soon as possible. Please advise President Chavez to expect a call. They will need to arrange a closed-door meeting with the member states of the United Nations as soon as possible. This needs to be dealt with on a global level quickly while keeping it away from the media. If the general public finds out we are under attack by aliens, all bets are off. We'll have mass hysteria around the world," said Secretary Laurent.

"I'll brief the president on our meeting and advise him to expect a call from President Dubois in the near future," responded Lyman.

After Lyman left, Secretary Laurent held a meeting with his officers and staff and briefed them on the situation. He also impressed upon them the importance of keeping this information closely guarded. "We need to determine the best method of monitoring the air to detect carbon dioxide and other pollutants that may be entering our atmosphere. Identify, but don't take any action against the perpetrators without running it through me first. We also need to devise a faster and more efficient way of identifying these alien lifeforms other than DNA testing. I want every store and shop in Paris that sells tanks containing CO_2 checked to see how many tanks were sold in the past six months and to who. Then we will need to set up a secure holding facility for the aliens once we identify them. We will also need professional interrogators to question them. Okay, get moving. I expect all team leaders to report back to me with any progress we make on this," said Laurent.

Chapter 19

Victor Obano was a second-generation ALF living in Lagos, Nigeria. His father had laid the groundwork for him by getting involved in politics and obtaining the position of minister of state for the environment. He had paved the way for his son to build and operate a factory in Lagos by approving all the necessary permits and regulatory documentation. This factory produced Freon for air-conditioning systems and aerosol sprays for a variety of purposes. Its four smokestacks pumped out large quantities of chlorofluorocarbons, which were being released into the atmosphere twenty-four hours a day, seven days a week. As they reached the stratosphere, the chlorine would interact with the ozone molecules, rendering them unable to block UVB rays from reaching Earth. This was in direct violation of the Montreal Protocol, but Victor had been paying off politicians to deny the factory was in violation. To make matters worse, these factories were powered by coal, the burning of which sent massive amounts of carbon dioxide into the atmosphere, accelerating the process of global warming.

Similar factories had been set up in Estrutural, Brazil; Mumbai, India; Pyongyang, North Korea; and cities in Myanmar, Somalia, and Nicaragua—all in impoverished areas where politicians could be bought and environmental regulations ignored. The chlorofluorocarbon emissions, carbon dioxide, and other pollutants that these factories were emitting would soon result in major climate change because of the resulting global warming as the greenhouse effect intensified.

This would be accompanied by a dramatic increase in cancer rates and other illnesses because of damage to the immune system and altered DNA structures as UVB exposure soars with the resulting loss of the ozone layer. Hurricanes would be more frequent and stronger. CO_2 levels would increase, and sea levels would rise as glaciers melted. All animal and plant life on Earth would begin dying off.

Victor had mixed feelings about his mission. His wife, Maria, was Nigerian and not an ALF, making his two daughters a mixed breed. Half human and half ALF, they had some unique health issues that confounded local doctors, and someday they might represent the majority of Earth's population. So much death and heartache lay ahead. Was it worth it to destroy one group of people so that another might survive? Victor had recently joined a growing group of ALFs through social media who were trying to find another solution to their problem, one that would allow for peaceful coexistence and an end to the factories and other attempts to duplicate the atmosphere of Veteris Orbis at the expense of the human race and other existing life-forms on Earth.

Daw Mya Seen was thirty-two and single and living in Naypyidaw, Myanmar. He was a major in the Army and in charge of the factories. Unlike his counterpart in Lagos, he had no misgivings about doing whatever was necessary to get his people here on Earth. He would gladly fight to the death to assure the success of the mission and the eradication of all these disgusting humans. The factories he supervised manufactured propellants for various aerosols and pumped ozone-killing pollutants into the stratosphere 24/7. He was very pleased with his contribution to the motherland and hoped to be handsomely rewarded for his efforts.

CHAPTER 20

Keith Shylock was a first-generation ALF who started his own news agency and built it up over the years until now it was the fourth-largest news corporation in the United States. It was called True News, and its agenda was that of the aliens—debunking global warming theories, playing down any environmental issues or concerns, and calling any alarms raised about the ozone layer as being silly and not based on scientific principles.

"Katie, these stories you're hearing on the liberal media about holes in the ozone layer and the consequences are absolutely ludicrous. Nature is very good at mending its own injuries and bouncing back. This world survived for millions of years before man arrived, and it will continue to survive long after we're all gone," said the self-professed expert during an interview on the True News Network. Zimmerman was nodding in approval as he watched.

Keith's background was carefully fabricated by High Command—birth certificates of his mother and father and two sisters, job history for his dad, and academic records for him and his sister. His dad was a high school dropout who had worked as a janitor for a time and drove a school bus for a couple of years, as well as other minimum-wage jobs to feed his family. Despite the family hardship, Keith did well in school and obtained a full scholarship to Wharton School of Business in New York, where he graduated with a degree in journalism. After working for a major newspaper as an

They're Here!!

editor for a few years, he obtained a loan from the Small Business Administration, hired a couple of reporters, and started his own news organization. Now twenty years, later he ran the fourth-largest television news network in the United States and devoted himself to championing conservative causes. His broadcasting catered to conservative religious groups, antiabortionists, and the National Rifle Association. While not openly supporting racists and homophobes, his network would rarely condemn them or their actions either.

Chapter 21

Thirty-year-old oceanographer Linda Clift was sitting in the break room at the McMurdo Antarctic Research Center on the south tip of Ross Island on the shore of McMurdo Sound in Antarctica. At five feet, four inches tall, with short blond hair and an athletic build under all those clothes, the men at the Center made good use of their imaginations in deciding what she looked like under all the thermal underwear, pants, jackets, scarf, and trapper hat. Her mittens were on the table next to her, and her hands were wrapped around a hot cup of black coffee.

Prior to coming to the Antarctic, she worked at the Woods Hole Oceanographic Institute in Falmouth, Massachusetts, where she got involved with another doctor working there. She thought she might be in love until he suddenly became enraged during what she considered a minor argument. After that, she broke off the relationship, but conditions at work became unbearable, and after work, she found him stalking her. So when the job in the Antarctic opened up, she jumped at it. She was six months into a one-year assignment with OASIIS (Observing and Understanding the Ocean below Antarctic Sea Ice and Ice Shelves). Her team's mission was to develop an observation system to study the ocean under the Antarctic sea ice and ice shelves. At 1.5 million square kilometers, this under-ice "blind spot" in the global ocean observing system was a major impediment to a better understanding of climate, biogeochemical cycles, and sea level rise.

She was fifteen minutes into a thirty-minute break before going back out to do some density and seismic testing of the ice shelf when Jason came in. Her boss, Jason Bowers, was ten years her senior, with rugged features, standing six feet, two inches, and built solid like a rock. Prematurely bald, he rarely took off his ski hat, and today was no exception as he came in and sat next to her. "How's it going today, Linda?" he started the conversation.

"Well, other than freezing my ass off every day and living like a nun surrounded by wolves, I'm doing just fine, Jason," she replied.

Jason just smiled and said, "Relax, Doctor, you're halfway through your tour, and the work you're doing will really make a difference in our understanding of global warming and the effects of ozone depletion."

"That may be, Jason," she replied, "but I wish you had an explanation for why our most sophisticated observation satellite went dark for nearly six months before I arrived here, while at the same time, we had unexplained seismic activity on a scale never before seen up here."

Jason was starting to look a little irritated when he said, "Look, we've been over this many times, Linda, and decided it probably had to do with solar flares."

"Well, I never bought into that theory, Jason," she retorted. "And I have another one you can chew on for a while."

"And what might that be?" said Jason.

"Ever hear of Operation Highjump?" she asked.

"Can't say that I have," he replied.

"Known as Task Force 68, it was a US Navy Antarctic expedition that was launched in early 1947 with Admiral Richard Byrd in command. It was made up of the aircraft carrier USS *Philippine Sea* and a number of naval support ships and aircraft comprising some 4,700 military personnel. Their six-month mission was to find and destroy a hidden Nazi base. The Nazis had established a presence in the Antarctic as far back as 1938, and in 1943, German Grand Admiral Karl Dönitz sent the following message to Hitler: 'The German submarine fleet is proud of having built for the Führer an impregnable fortress.' After the defeat of Nazi Germany, according to various sources, elite Nazi scientists and leaders escaped to this impregnable fortress by U-boats. So the objective of Operation Highjump was to find and destroy this fortress. But on the way, they encountered a mysterious UFO force that attacked them, destroying several ships and a significant number of planes.

"According to eyewitness accounts, 'The UFOs shot vertically out of the water at tremendous velocity, as though pursued by the devil.' When the navy ships fired on them, the UFOs retaliated with deadly effects. This was the first-known historical incident involving a battle between US naval forces and an unknown UFO force and is chronicled in a 2006 Russian documentary. Initial press reports from Chile did indeed state that Operation Highjump had suffered 'many casualties.' So just maybe the impregnable fortress is under the ice shelf below us and aliens are living there," she said, half kidding. "Or maybe all this snow and ice is just making me crazy. But something just doesn't feel right," she concluded as she rose, put her mittens back on and her hood up, and disappeared out the door, back to the wind and snow.

Jason's expression said he was not amused.

CHAPTER 22

Rick Spence was an astronomer working with the SETI (Search for Extraterrestrial Intelligence) Institute. He was monitoring the Allen Telescope Array (ATA) at Hat Creek Radio Observatory in California while some upgrades were being done, which would enable it to detect a wider variety of wavelengths coming from deep space. The system was shut down while the upgrades were done.

"Well, Janice," he said to his assistant, Janice Joplin, as he leaned back in his office chair with his hands on the back of his head, "what do you think we'll see when we turn the system back on and boot up? A flotilla of alien ships converging upon us or maybe just a new signal saying, 'Is anybody out there?'" He laughed.

"Hopefully, we will hear from whatever planet you came from explaining what kind of life-form you are," she responded playfully.

Just then, the job foreman opened the door and said, "Okay, Rick, it's all yours. Power that baby up and enjoy your new toy."

About an hour later, after running diagnostics and checking the various systems out, they were ready to go online.

"Be my guest, Jan," said Rick. "It's only fitting that you should be the first one to speak to my home planet."

With that, Janice hit the Enter key. They both sat there looking at the screen as it flicked through various stages and then settled in and stayed at the screen they were used to seeing.

"The least they could have done was add some gaming software so we wouldn't be so bored around here," Rick complained.

Then it happened. The screen started flashing, and the alarm went off. They both looked at the screen and said at the same time, "Holy shit!"

Chapter 23

Lyman was on his way to Charles de Gaulle Airport to catch a flight to Washington when another call from Lattimer came in. "What's up, Tom?" answered Lyman.

"I'll get right to the point, Lyman. We need you to head for the Antarctic. The Allen Telescope Array at the Hat Creek Radio Observatory picked up an alien communications signal coming from deep space. About 94 million light-years away actually. It's aimed just north of the McMurdo Antarctic Research Center in the Antarctic. You're booked on a flight tomorrow morning out of CDG to Buenos Aires, where a helicopter will pick you up and take you out to rendezvous with the USS *Hampton*. The *Hampton* is a Los Angeles class nuclear submarine. It will take you to the McMurdo Antarctic Research Center. Your contact at the center will be Linda Clift. For security reasons, she is the only one who knows you are coming and has the exact coordinates and time the *Hampton* will be surfacing. You need to find out who is receiving these signals from 94 million light-years away and exactly where the receiver is located. This must be the command and control center for these things, and we can't make a plan of attack until we know where we are going."

"Well, I guess I'll go find a hotel near the airport here and rest up for the trip. Looks like I'm going to need a good night's sleep," said Lyman as he ended the call.

CHAPTER 24

Captain Frederick Thayer was standing in the control room with Lyman Shore next to him as the USS *Hampton* cruised along the Ross Island coastline en route to the McMurdo Antarctic Research Station at a depth of ten meters. "How you feeling, Lyman?" the captain asked.

"Not too bad, Captain. I've been locked up in a tank before. This is a little roomier than that was. Almost there?" asked Lyman.

"We'll be scanning the area through the periscope soon. Assuming we find your ride waiting for you at the agreed-upon coordinates and all looks good, we'll surface and get you on your way. Better grab your stuff and be ready, Deputy."

Sitting in her Tucker Sno-Cat overlooking Ross Sound, Linda Clift was scanning the ocean in front of her. The coordinates Special Agent Lattimer gave her were about two hundred yards directly in front of her, smack in the middle of the ocean. It was minus twenty-three degrees centigrade or about minus ten degrees Fahrenheit with a light three-mile-per-hour wind out of the southeast. Suddenly, she witnessed this huge black metallic whale rising up from the depths of the ocean.

Lyman Shore climbed up and into the Tucker Sno-Cat, closed the door, and looked over to Linda Clift. The cabin temperature was comfortable, and Linda's face was not covered. Lyman was struck by her silky short blond hair and deep blue eyes, and he felt a bit intimidated as his heart rate accelerated in spite of himself. Lyman grew up with two brothers and was not as comfortable around a beautiful woman as someone who might have grown up with sisters. "Good afternoon," he simply said.

Linda had been sizing up Lyman since he climbed out of the dingy, grabbed his duffel bag, and made his way to the Sno-Cat from the submarine, noting his strong, determined stride through the snow. Once inside the cab, she was taken by his hazel eyes and rugged facial features. For some reason, she felt immediately at ease and comfortable with this man who seemed so strong and yet shy. *Get ahold of yourself, Linda,* she thought to herself. *Remember, the last time you thought you had found the right man for you, he ended up being an abusive stalker.* "Good afternoon, Marshal Shore," she replied.

"Please, make it Lyman. If we're going to endure this inhospitable climate together, we should at least use first names. And I believe yours is Linda," he said.

"Yes, and now that we got that out of the way, can you enlighten me as to why your arrival is such a secret that only I could know about it?"

Lyman paused as he was caught staring. Her gestures, mannerisms, and little quirks as she spoke mesmerized him.

"Hello," she said.

Lyman snapped out of it quickly. "Look, can we go to your hut or something and get comfortable, and I'll tell you all about it," he finally said.

Linda had a small room to herself with bunk beds, a small sofa, a desk, and a TV in the main dormitory. It was wintertime, and about two hundred personnel were currently living and working at McMurdo. "This is my hut," she jokingly said as she opened the door. "You will have the one across the hall while you're here," she said as she handed him the key. "Come on in and have a seat," she continued, motioning to the love seat while she hung her jacket up in the small wardrobe closet.

Lyman threw his jacket on the sofa and sat down while Linda sat on the bottom bunk, facing him.

"So let's have it," she said.

Lyman started at the beginning and filled her in, finishing with the signal from deep space.

"Holy shit, Operation Highjump was real," she declared.

"What?" asked Lyman.

"Never mind. Are you sure this isn't some kind of sick cosmic joke you're playing on me?" she asked, staring at Lyman with those damned blue eyes of hers.

"I wish it were, Linda," he said. "Sometimes I wonder if it's all just a bad dream and I'm going to wake up any minute. But I'm afraid it's all too real. Now I'm going to go across the hall and get some sleep while you digest all that I have told you. I have the exact coordinates where the signal is contacting Earth. It's about three miles northeast of here, and you and I are going there in the morning to investigate," he said as he left, closing the door behind him.

Jason Bowers stood in an all-white hooded thermal jumpsuit, blending in with the snow, about two hundred yards from the dormitory, watching as the Sno-Cat carrying Linda and Lyman pull up to the dormitory. He watched them get out and go into the building. Then he got into his snowmobile and headed off to the northeast at full throttle.

Chapter 25

The next morning, Lyman was knocking on Linda's door at 5:30 a.m. He expected to see her at her worst when she opened the door. She was wearing baby-blue pajamas, hair tousled, eyes half closed, and no makeup, yet she was still beautiful.

"What the hell time do US Marshals usually have breakfast?" she asked, squinting up at him in the lighted hallway.

"Thought you Antarctic researchers were early-to-bed-and-early-to-rise types," he countered with a smile.

"Well, there's early, and then there's in the middle of the night. Go back to your little room, and I'll come and get you when I look and feel human," she responded.

"Okay," he said, although she looked just fine to him.

"Come on, Mr. Marshal Man," Linda said through Lyman's door thirty minutes later. "I'll buy you breakfast." She was bundled up for the short walk to the cafeteria, but Lyman still had a hard time not staring at her as they walked through the snow.

"So what drives a woman like you to want to live up here in this frozen tundra?" he asked.

"Well, that's a sexist question if I ever heard one," she replied with a smile.

"Sorry, I suppose you're right," he said. "It just seems like the choices for after-work entertainment are a bit limited here. Not to mention a limited list of good restaurants and such in the area."

Lyman opened the door to the cafeteria and stepped aside, motioning Linda to enter.

"Such chivalry," she said as she went inside. "So what's the plan?" Linda asked as they sat down with their breakfast from the buffet line.

"We load up the Sno-Cat and head on over to the coordinates Lattimer gave me and see what we can see," he said.

Thirty minutes later, Lyman was in his room assembling the AR-15 he had in his duffel, and just as he inserted the magazine, Linda knocked on the door. "Ready to take a ride," he said as he opened the door with the duffel over his right shoulder and the AR-15 in his left hand.

"You expecting trouble?" Linda asked, looking at the rifle.

"Just a precaution," replied Lyman. Lyman didn't know what to expect but wanted to be prepared for anything.

Since Brenda died, he had been shut down when it came to the ladies. Something inside him died with her. But when he stepped into that Sno-Cat and saw Linda sitting there, everything suddenly changed. It was like Brenda was in his head, saying, "It's okay, baby. She's what you need. Go find some happiness. I love you." He was gonna make damn sure she was safe, whatever it took. He had a four-power scope, a hundred rounds of ammunition, a half-dozen grenades, and a satellite radio in his duffel, along with a small shovel and a halogen flashlight.

Soon they were driving northeast across the ice shelf at thirty miles an hour and would arrive where the scientists determined the deep space signal was contacting Earth in about five minutes. It had not snowed overnight, and they noticed they were following what appeared to be snowmobile tracks in front of them.

"Anyone you know had reason to be out this way recently?" Lyman asked.

"Could be one of our researchers checking something out or someone just taking a joy ride. I wouldn't worry too much," she replied.

"Well, slow down. According to my GPS, we're just about there," said Lyman.

They're Here!!

The snowmobile tracks continued up a slope, and about two hundred yards away, Lyman caught a glimpse of glare as the sun reflected off something metallic. He instinctively reached over with his left hand and pushed the steering column to the left, swinging the Snow-Cat hard in that direction. A bullet exploded through the right-side passenger window and exited out the left-side rear window as the Snow-Cat came to a stop in the snow.

"Out!" Lyman yelled as Linda opened the door while Lyman pushed her out and followed close behind. They landed hard on the snow as two more bullets slammed into the right side of the vehicle. "Lay facedown and stay down," he said to Linda and then opened the rear door and grabbed the AR-15 that was lying on the seat with one hand and reached into the duffel and pulled out the scope with the other. He snapped the scope onto the top of the barrel and crawled under the truck and set the sight on the top of the slope. Snow was getting kicked up in front of him, and other rounds were loudly snapping into the metal side of the Sno-Cat. The scope was sighted in for a one-hundred-yard distance with no wind. The wind was coming from the east at about four or five miles per hour, so he aimed a little high and just a hair to the left of where the muzzle flashes were coming from. Then he fired six quick rounds in a small imaginary circle and saw the snow kicking up around where the fire was coming from. Then silence. He waited a few seconds and then fired three more rounds. Nothing.

"You okay?" Lyman asked as he crawled out from under the truck.

"Yes, other than having the shit scared out of me," Linda replied.

"Okay, here's what we're going to do. You get in and drive very slowly up the slope with your head down, keeping the right side of the truck between you and the shooter. I'm going to walk behind using the truck for cover and keep my aim on the position where the fire was coming from. Keep your head down, and if you hear any gunfire, stop and jump out. If there is no fire, then keep driving slowly until I tell you to stop. Got it?"

"Got it," she said and crawled up into the driver's seat.

There was no gunfire, and when they got to the top of the ridge, Linda heard Lyman say, "Stop." When she got out, she saw Lyman standing over a body facedown in the snow with an AK-47 still in his hands. He knelt down, rolled the figure onto its back, pulled off the face mask, and said, "You know this guy?"

"Yes," she said stoically. "That's my boss, Jason Bowers."

"And that must be his ride," Lyman said, motioning to the snowmobile about ten yards away. "We need to load this body into the Sno-Cat until I can figure out what to do with it," he said.

Chapter 26

"Okay, someone obviously did not want us here. But the fact remains that we are here, and this alien communication signal is contacting Earth just down that slope," Lyman said as they sat in the Sno-Cat after loading Bowers's body in the back. What's underneath us there?" Lyman asked.

"Lyman, you are standing on the Ross Ice Shelf of Antarctica. It covers about 188,000 miles, which is about the size of France. The ice here is about 3 feet thick, and then the ocean goes down another 1,000 feet or so. My mission here was to establish an under-ice observation system to enable us to see what's going on in this huge blind spot in the global ocean system, thereby improving our understanding of climate, weather cycles, and sea level rise," Linda said.

"We believe there is an alien command and control center down there, and we need to find it," said Lyman. "How do we get down there?"

"You don't," said Linda. "But I have an idea. Seals are the only animals of any size who routinely navigate those waters. We have captured one and placed a camera and some other instruments on her in an effort to gather information on some of the unexplored areas under the ice shelf. We could bring her out here and cut a hole in the ice and send her in to see what she can find. It seems a bit ironic that just the other morning, I was telling Mr. Bowers there about Operation Highjump, and now you show up." Linda went on to explain what Operation Highjump was and about the 2006 Russian documentary, the UFO battle, and the admiral's claim to have built a fortress. "The second possibility is, it was just built in the past year by alien forces who managed to shut down an observation satellite for six months before my arrival here. During those six months, seismic activity was noted. That could have been caused by the construction of the command post. Then suddenly, the satellite comes back online and the seismic activity stops. Either way, I would bet my bullet-riddled Sno-Cat that something is down there," Linda said.

"Well, that's quite a story, Linda. Considering the road I've been down lately, I'm open to any and all theories. How about you work on getting that seal ready, and I'll call Lattimer on the SAT phone and tell him what we've got here," said Lyman.

Chapter 27

About eight hundred feet below where Lyman and Linda sat in the Sno-Cat, Commander Orion Dorlestor stood in the center of the Global Command and Control Center, looking out of the glass that surrounded him on all four sides. He could see urchins, sea spiders, anemone, and seals. Once in a while, a huge leopard seal would come into view, but they couldn't see him. The Command Center was camouflaged, so anyone or anything looking at it from the ocean would just see more water as if nothing was there. Only by actually bumping into it would you know it existed. He had just witnessed the firefight above thanks to the drone he had positioned over the area.

"This Lyman Shore is proving to be a worthy opponent and a real annoyance, Captain," he said to his second in command standing next to him.

"It seems we just lost a third soldier, thanks to him, with Mr. Bowers's unfortunate demise. Since we don't seem to be having any success in killing him, find out who or what matters most to him and let's find a way to get him off our backs. It's been over seventy years since we first arrived on Earth from Veteris Orbis. After three generations, we have managed to install people in positions of authority and power in countries on seven continents. The Montreal Protocol was a setback, but we seem to be back on track now and are on schedule for the removal of 60 percent of the ozone molecules in the stratosphere in the next twelve to twenty-four months. This will start the process to make Earth more compatible for our people, while most of the native population will die within months. We can then transport the population of Veteris Orbis to their new home here on Earth. So let's get this Shore character taken care of before he causes any more problems."

Before leaving the site of the alien signal, Lyman got Lattimer on the SAT phone. "Hello, Lattimer," said Lyman. "We made it out to the site that the deep space signal is going to. Nothing visible there but snow and ice. The ice is three feet thick with a thousand feet of ocean below it. Ms. Clift has managed to place a camera on a seal and will release it through a hole in the ice near the signal location and hopefully get lucky. One more thing, we were greeted upon our arrival with gunfire from an AK-47. The shooter is now deceased and needs a ride to Dallas, where he can be properly studied," Lyman finished.

"Holy shit, Lyman. Was anyone else injured?" Lattimer replied.

"No, I got lucky and caught the glare of the sun coming off the barrel just before he fired. I was able to take evasive action just in time," explained Lyman.

"Good work, Lyman. I'll contact Captain Thayer and have him resurface at the same location at 1600 Zulu and pick up the package," said Lattimer.

"Sounds like a plan, boss," said Lyman and hung up. "Okay, Linda, you better take the snowmobile, and I'll follow you back to the dormitory and then continue on to deliver your boss to Captain Thayer. When I get back, we'll need to either cover the truck or garage it somewhere. I'd rather not have to explain how all the bullet holes got there. Tell any interested parties that Mr. Bowers had to return to the States for a family emergency. Then we can see about getting the site ready for the seal's arrival."

CHAPTER 28

Julie Emmons was an undergraduate student now in her senior year at Yale University, majoring in political science. It was a daunting task trying to understand what happened in this country in the last sixty years or so. In the 1950s, over 50 percent of the American people felt they could trust the federal government. Today that was 17 percent. Fifty percent of the population today get their news from social media where anyone could say anything—lies, half-truths, innuendos, and comments taken out of context and manipulated to say the opposite of what was intended. Right and wrong, black and white. No compromise or meaningful, respectful debate. No effort to determine the truth. And when faced with facts that do not support your preconceived opinions, then that's just fake news. Why do people just not care when the president and cabinet members continually make proven false statements to the American people? Where is the accountability? Why do we not demand integrity, honesty, and ethical behavior from the people we elect to represent us? It was a truly depressing yet fascinating time to be studying political science.

When Julie got the word that her father was missing and presumed dead, she couldn't believe it. And the stories about the gambling and the mob? Her dad had never been a gambler. He was a levelheaded scientist and mathematician who knew all too well that the odds were against you. The stories she read in the papers made no sense, but no one seemed interested in what she had to say. This fictional account of her father got better ratings than any factual account would get. She was devastated by the loss. She was always Daddy's little girl growing up and spoiled rotten. He would hoist her up on his shoulders and swing her around and take her everywhere. She always felt her mom was jealous of their relationship somehow. Then when her mom got sick, their lives were turned upside down. She was only ten and devastated but also knew her dad was having a real hard time dealing with it, and when her mom died, she felt it was her job to keep her dad together. Then a few years later, when she went away to Yale, they would message or FaceTime at least once a week. She really missed him.

She was in her dormitory room at her desk, reading "Republicans—from Buckley to Trump—What Happened?" by William Traverse, when someone knocked on her door. She opened the door to find a tall man in a dark suit on the other side.

"Ms. Emmons?" he asked. "Yes," she replied.

"I'm Special Agent Tom Lattimer with the FBI. May I come in?"

CHAPTER 29

FBI director James Kalahar was at his office in Washington, DC, when he got a call from Secretary of Commerce Alan Cromwell. "Good morning, Al. How's the golf game going?" asked Kalahar.

"Still working on breaking ninety, Jim. Hopefully, it will happen before I turn ninety." He laughed. "Look, Jim, I got a call from Fred Jacobs over at the NOAA. He's in charge of the Global Monitoring Division of the Earth System Research Laboratory. They have recently detected large quantities of CFCs and CO_2 emissions entering the atmosphere from Brazil, India, Myanmar, Somalia, Nicaragua, and North Korea. If these emissions continue at the current rate, it could have catastrophic consequences to the planet as a result of ozone depletion and accelerated global warming," he said.

"Okay, Al, I'm going to call Secretary of Staff Bishop and see when we can get in to see the president. I'll need you and Fred Jacobs to put together a presentation for him. Hopefully, we can convince him of the gravity of the situation and devise a plan of action. I'll get back to you when the meeting is arranged," replied Kalahar. "Oh, and, Al, please keep this information strictly between us. No need for the attorney general or anyone else to know about it yet," he added.

"Okay, Jim, I look forward to hearing back from you. Goodbye," said Cromwell as he hung up.

Kalahar pushed the intercom button. "Nancy, call the office of the secretary of staff and request a meeting with the president as soon as possible. Tell him the secretary of commerce and some of his staff members will be attending and that it is concerning an environmental issue of crucial importance. Also, request a separate private meeting with the president following that meeting," he said.

"Yes, sir," replied his secretary.

He would brief the president privately on Shore's meeting with the secretary general of INTERPOL in France and tell him to expect a call from President Dubois. Kalahar then sat quietly at his desk, going over the day's events in his mind. *I can only hope the president is not an ALF,* he thought.

CHAPTER 30

Gary Shore was a successful certified public accountant (CPA) with offices in Daytona Beach and Ormond Beach, Florida. He didn't see much of his younger brother Lyman in recent years, but the brotherly bond was strong, and they remained close in their own way. His wife, Carol, ran the Daytona Beach office, and Gary managed the Ormond Beach one. He lived alone in his sixth-floor condo overlooking the Atlantic, while Carol lived in the house in Daytona with her sixteen-year-old son Robert. He was her child from a previous marriage and showed little respect for Carol. One day when Robert was being particularly rude to Carol, Gary stepped in and grabbed him by the throat and said, "Listen, you little shit. If you like your head attached to your shoulders, you'll apologize to your mother." Carol stepped in and told Gary to let him go and told Robert to just go to his room. While he loved Carol, he wasn't going to live in the same house with a spoiled teenager he had no control over. The next day, he moved into the condo in Ormond Beach.

The two ALFs who were sent to pick up Gary Shore in Ormond Beach were parked on the other side of US Highway 1 across from Gary's condo building. They knew his 2014 Toyota Seneca would be leaving at 7:00 a.m. this morning, just as it had every morning for the last four mornings. He would stop at Starbucks for a cup of coffee and read the paper before going into the office. He was a creature of habit who they had followed for the past week. But he would not make it to Starbucks today. They would take him quietly at gunpoint when he got out of his car at Starbucks. There orders were to take him to a local motel and hold him until further instructions were given. His life or death would depend on his brother Lyman. This was just a forty-four-year-old accountant, and they were not worried or expecting any difficulty in picking him up.

What they didn't know was that Gary Shore had spent three years in the US Army Ranger program, during which time he was in Black Ops missions throughout the world. He was highly trained and had stayed in shape since his discharge. Aware of their tail on him since day 1, he had been watching them watch him. Now he was looking at them from behind the building on the ocean side. He was on his cell phone with Florida State Police Officer Stan Flaherty. Stan had served in the Marine Corps in Iraq and Afghanistan and met Gary at the local VFW about a year earlier. "Stan, these two jokers have been following me for four days now. They are parked on the other side of US 1, waiting for me to drive out of the parking garage. They're in a red Toyota Camry rental. Be careful approaching them. They're probably armed."

The ALFs watched the state police cruiser drive by, do a U-turn, and pull up behind them as the red-and-blue flashing lights went on. The driver put the Camry in gear and took off down US Highway 1. Gary ran across the highway and jumped in the cruiser, and the pursuit was on. Officer Flaherty radioed his position in and that he was in pursuit southbound on US 1. The Camry passed several vehicles, and with traffic congestion and traffic lights, Officer Flaherty lost sight of it and deemed it unsafe to the local population to continue the pursuit. Flaherty turned off the lights and siren and put out an APB for the Camry. The car was found abandoned a few hours later.

Chapter 31

Lyman was about to leave with Linda to drill a hole in the ice for Sabrina (the seal) at the site they believed to be above the alien command post when his satellite phone rang. "Hello," he said.

"Hello, Lyman. How's everything in your winter paradise up—oops—down there?" Lattimer asked with a chuckle.

"An FBI comedian, now there's an oxymoron for you," countered Lyman.

"Look, Lyman. Two things—first, your brother Gary called your office looking for you. It appears that a couple of ALFs may have been planning on abducting him, or worse, but he spotted them and called the police, and they're on the run now," Lattimer said.

"Looks like they're going after anyone close to me now," replied Lyman. "This just got personal."

"The second reason I called is because Dr. Emmons and his team finished studying some of our recently deceased friends from the ALF community and has come up with a theory. I thought it best if we all hear it at the same time," Lattimer continued.

"Linda is here with me, so I'll put you on speaker. Okay, let's have it," replied Lyman.

"Lyman, this is Dr. Emmons. As you know, we found high levels of carbon dioxide in the blood of all the aliens, and they were all found to be wearing contact lenses. Now we have determined the contacts have the effect of increasing the amount of UVB rays being absorbed. Okay, so I have been trying to figure out where these folks came from, and this is the best theory I can come up with. At some point, perhaps a million years or more in the past, these people were living on a planet similar to Earth.

"Just like us, they reached a stage in their history where they industrialized and started throwing large amounts of chlorine, carbon dioxide, and other pollutants into the air. But they did not realize the consequences of their actions or did not have the political will to make the necessary changes to protect their environment. So they obliterated their ozone layer with the chlorine and bromide while at the same time trapping carbon dioxide and other air pollutants in the stratosphere, creating the perfect storm of global warming and UVB radiation saturation. A snowball effect followed with the warming of the oceans, leading to drought, which led to fires that destroyed their rain forests, which caused billions of metric tons of carbon dioxide to be released into the atmosphere. In the end, most animal life on the surface and sea life down to a certain depth was eradicated.

"Slowly, over a million or millions of years, their planet repaired itself. New life emerged as the process of evolution worked its magic once again, and a new breed of *Homo sapiens* emerged. They evolved in a world with approximately 40 percent of the ozone we have here on Earth and much higher levels of carbon dioxide in their air. Fast-forward a few thousand more years and they have thrived and advanced technologically. But now perhaps because of overpopulation or a dying sun, they need somewhere else to go. So what we are looking at is the advanced party to get this planet ready for habitation. Look for anyone who keeps bottled CO_2 nearby. If they don't keep the CO_2 levels up in their blood, they will suffer pulmonary oxygen toxicity, lung damage, and death. I hope this information helps," Emmons concluded.

"Thank you, Doctor," said Lyman. "It definitely helps to know your enemy."

That evening, Lyman sat in his room trying to absorb all the information Emmons had given him and to understand how it fit into everything else he had learned. He browsed the Internet to have a better understanding of global warming and ozone depletion. Then something struck him, and he got Dr. Emmons back on the phone. "Hello, Doctor. Sorry to bother you at this late hour, but I need to ask some questions and go over some things with you," said Lyman.

"No problem, Deputy. I couldn't sleep anyway," replied Emmons.

"Doctor, you said the air the aliens breathe on their home planet has 2 percent more carbon dioxide and 2 percent less oxygen, correct?" Lyman asked.

"That is my theory, yes," Emmons replied.

"And that if the aliens here did not get supplemental CO_2 to bring those levels up after a day of breathing our air, they could suffer pulmonary oxygen toxicity, lung damage, and death, correct?" Lyman queried.

"Yes, that's right," answered Emmons.

"When Drake and I went to New Jersey and looked at Mankewitz's body, the coroner told us the cause of death was a pulmonary embolism caused by a blood clot in one of the lungs. Does that sound like something that could be the result of oxygen toxicity?" asked Lyman.

"Yes, absolutely," said Emmons.

"Thank you, Doctor. You've been a big help," said Lyman.

"No problem. Anytime," said Emmons as they ended the call.

CHAPTER 32

The DNA of Director Phillip Harris came back human, and he was subsequently briefed by Ferguson and brought up to date on the situation. He had completed his investigation regarding who had given up Mankewitz and found the informant. Lucy Bainbridge was a deputy marshal who happened to be in the director's office on an unrelated matter when the call came in regarding the Texas governor and Mankewitz. Director Harris had exhausted all other leads when he remembered this and wondered what she might have overheard. She was brought in for questioning and appeared nervous and on edge. A forensic analysis was done on her laptop and evidence found that she had in fact discovered the address of Mankewitz and passed that information on to an IP address in Arlington, Virginia. That IP address was traced to the laptop belonging to Attorney General Kenneth Zimmerman. This information was given to Ferguson, who passed it on to FBI director James Kalahar just in time for his meeting with President Donaldo Sedillo Chavez.

Chapter 33

Malcolm Ferguson was excited as he waited for Lyman to pick up the satellite phone.

"Hello," Lyman answered.

"Deputy Shore, this is Special Agent Ferguson. Great news, we finally broke Castoro down, and he has started talking. He pretty much verifies what we already know but has also given us some valuable new information. The alien's home planet is called Veteris Orbis, and its sun is in fact dying, so Professor Emmons was right on with that theory. The other interesting thing is, they have no military capability. They did away with individual nations hundreds of years ago. The entire planet is one country, so there are no enemies to worry about, hence no need to waste resources on weapons. Of course, they have a planetary police force who have weapons to maintain order and such. This is where they drew from for the soldier element sent here to Earth. And they have defensive weapons on the home planet and on their space vessels to destroy comets or asteroids that may pose a threat. But they have been able to devote their resources for the most part to further science and technology and make their planet a better place to live.

"They are very proficient at space travel and have learned to use wormholes to transport themselves many hundreds of light-years to find other habitable planets. We can only guess at what other technological advances they may have made. But according to Castoro,

Earth is not the only planet being made ready for their departure from Veteris Orbis. There are apparently several others being prepared to receive the exodus. So they don't have all their eggs in one basket, and we are hoping if we can make this difficult enough for them, they might just be persuaded to move on," Ferguson finished.

Lyman took a minute to digest the new information and then said, "Malcolm, something has been bothering me about all this. Let me ask you. Was Mankewitz's DNA taken and analyzed?"

"Well, let me think. I don't think we saw any need. He was clearly terrified of Castoro and told us about the phone call he overheard of Castoro talking to someone about the alien invasion. Certainly, he would not offer that information if he were himself an ALF," Ferguson said.

"What if it was all a big show to throw us off in one direction while they concentrate on another? We need to have Mankewitz's DNA tested as soon as possible. The coroner in Newark, New Jersey, should have tissue samples taken during the autopsy," said Lyman.

"Okay, I'll get it done and get back to you." said Ferguson, and the call ended.

Chapter 34

Lyman and Linda were sitting in the Tucker Sno-Cat watching the video feed in real time. Sabrina was about eight hundred feet down now. They saw some giant sea spiders, urchins, giant sea stars, shellfish, soft corals and sponges, and forests of kelp. What they didn't see was anything that remotely looked like a command post or anything, for that matter, that looked like it didn't belong there.

"So why is a signal from 94 million light-years away ending up here?" Lyman said more to himself than to Linda.

* * * * *

Commander Orion Dorlestor stood watching the seal with the camera attached swim by for the fifth time. On the monitor, he was also watching the Sno-Cat parked in the snow above them. He had just gotten the news that the two soldier ALFs sent to pick up Lyman's brother had blown their cover and botched that job also. Captain ZReubnth, second in command and whose name is not pronounceable in English, stood beside him.

"Captain, this mission is in peril. Mr. Shore is continuing to cause problems for us, and that trait seems to have spread over to his brother. We have underestimated both of them to our detriment, I'm afraid. It's been over seventy years since we sent the first hundred thousand brothers and sisters through the wormhole to establish identities and set down roots on this planet. They became reputable citizens on every continent, becoming tradesmen, doctors, entrepreneurs, politicians, and working families.

"Soon fifty thousand more were sent to be the soldiers responsible for dealing with problems that arose if the locals became suspicious. They were anonymous and expendable volunteers who could not be traced back to any of our professional brethren. We have our people embedded in every profession today and have successfully influenced policy decisions to debunk global warming theories and ozone depletion paranoia throughout the world. We now have the factories up and running and will have Earth ready to accommodate all of our people in a few short years as the native population expires and we take control.

"But this has only worked because of its covert nature. If the general public is made aware of our presence too soon, then all bets are off, and I'm afraid the gentlemen in the truck above us just might make that happen. I may have to take care of him myself," Dorlestor said.

* * * * *

"Have you noticed something about this video, Linda?" asked Lyman as they continued to observe Sabrina.

"What do you mean?" she replied.

"Look, she seems to go out the same distance and then turns as if running parallel to something for a while and then coming back. She has done that pattern four times in a row now," he said.

"Are you saying something might be there and we just can't see it and her instruments can't pick it up either?" Linda asked.

"If these folks came here from 94 million light-years away, who knows what technology they brought with them. The next time she makes that turn, let's lock in those GPS coordinates. I'm going to see if we can arrange a ride on the USS *Hampton*," Lyman replied. "I have a feeling the guy who wants me dead so bad is behind door number 1, and that invisible door is directly in front of Sabrina. He's probably

They're Here!!

watching Sabrina right now. I might have viewed him as just a soldier trying to do his job until he sent his goons to get my brother. That made it personal, and I intend to rain on his little parade."

CHAPTER 35

Attorney General Zimmerman was home at 8:00 p.m. when he put on his coat and said to his wife in the adjoining room, "Honey, I have a meeting with the FBI director. I shouldn't be too long."

"Okay, be careful, and I'll see you in a little while," she replied. She was not surprised since he had been going to late-night appointments for some time now. *Such is the life of a high government official involved in law enforcement during these troubled and violent times,* she thought to herself.

But he had no meeting with the FBI director. He was going to an abandoned warehouse outside of the city. When he got there, he saw about a hundred vehicles parked in an open field across from the warehouse. There were no exterior lights on as he parked quietly in the field, walked across to the building, opened the door, and went inside. There were about two hundred men and women mingling together in the big building. Most of them were armed with side pistols, and a few had assault rifles. There was a small stage at one end, and a microphone was set up in the center of it on a podium. Zimmerman stepped up to it.

"Good evening, my brave soldiers," he said.

They all roared back at him in unison, "Good evening!"

"You will notice the chart to my left. You will step up and find your number on this chart, and next to your number will be your target and a date. This is the date your target must die. It should be done

They're Here!!

as quietly and with the least amount of fanfare and, if possible, made to look like an accident or death by natural causes. We have people in place who are in a good position to replace these folks, and this will allow our agenda to move forward more quickly. So line up, find your target, and quietly leave to make your plans," Zimmerman finished.

Just then, the exterior around the building was lit up like a ballpark, and through a loudspeaker, they heard, "This is the FBI. The building is surrounded. Come out in single file with your hands on top of your head with fingers crossed."

As Kalahar watched from outside, the door swung open. He had been monitoring Zimmerman's communications on Messenger as well as his email and knew of this meeting in advance. There were fifty heavily armed FBI agents waiting in the nearby woods for Zimmerman to arrive, and as soon as he went inside, they set up to cover the exits. Their demand was met with silence. Then suddenly, the ALFs came running out in single file and firing their weapons. The FBI opened up with automatic weapons. When it was over, there were 137 dead and 71 wounded, and the attorney general was taken into custody.

Kalahar and the people from the Department of Commerce had met with President Chavez two days earlier and briefed him on everything. In his private meeting with the president, Kalahar had submitted the evidence of Zimmerman being an ALF and the one responsible for Mankewitz's death. President Chavez gave him the authority to follow Zimmerman and take whatever action he deemed necessary in the best interest of the country up to and including arrest and incarceration of the attorney general. The names on that chart inside the warehouse included the president and the FBI director.

President Chavez was the first Hispanic American president, and since his election, America's relations with Central American and South American nations had improved considerably. He would spend today calling the leaders of the countries who were operating factories in violation of the Montreal Protocol and insist they shut them down immediately under threat of unilateral sanctions and/or possible military action.

Chapter 36

"This is Holly Jacobs reporting for ABC News. Scientists have recently discovered new holes in the ozone layer over Southeast Asia and South America. ABC News has learned that the Global Monitoring Division of the Commerce Department recently found factories in six countries were releasing large quantities of chlorofluorocarbons into the atmosphere in violation of the Montreal Protocol. The Montreal Protocol, finalized in 1987, is a global agreement to protect the stratospheric ozone layer by phasing out the production and consumption of ozone-depleting substances [ODS]. The discovery of these factories could explain why cancer rates and illnesses related to weakened immune systems have soared in recent months. A source close to the White House tells us that President Chavez has been on the phone with the leaders of these countries in an effort to shut down those factories."

Commander Dorlestor turned off the television in the hotel room. He transported himself from the command post to the room in the Capital Hilton upon hearing about the disaster at the warehouse and subsequent arrest of Zimmerman. "Ladies and gentlemen," he addressed his top twenty lieutenants from the soldier division in the room, "we suffered our greatest losses yesterday since our initial arrival here. We are here to honor their sacrifice and make plans for moving forward. Apparently, the American government is aware of our presence here. However, the news has not broken about the shoot-out at the warehouse, and that tells me they don't want the public to know. Talk of alien invasion and such might spread panic through the population, so they would prefer to keep this little battle under the radar, so to speak.

"Those of you in the media business will have to cast doubt on the validity of this Montreal Protocol violation and debunk and discredit the Global Monitoring Division of the Commerce Department. Go after the whole ozone thing as made-up science and fake news and show it in the light of a powerful and rich country like the United States going after poor countries whose people need the jobs associated with these harmless factories. The rest of you, go on social media and do the same thing, that President Chavez was attacking these poor countries and taking jobs away instead of giving them much-needed foreign aid. The rest of you, talk to your coworkers and get public opinion moving in the right direction. The longer we can keep those factories running, the closer we will get to completing our mission here. That's all for now. I will be monitoring your progress from here. You're dismissed," he said, concluding his speech.

Chapter 37

"Ladies and gentlemen, it appears we have a global crisis on our hands," President Chavez said as he began the meeting. The attendees were director of the FBI, James Kalahar; associate director for operations for the US Marshals Service, Phillip Harris; FBI special agent in charge of the Dallas office, Malcolm Ferguson; FBI Special Agent Tom Lattimer; FBI Special Agent Jim Fredericks; geneticist Dr. James T. Emmons; Mr. Drake Borden with the Texas governor's office; US Deputy Marshal Lyman Shore; and oceanographer Linda Clift.

"Last week, Director Kalahar briefed me on this critical situation we find ourselves in. Normally, when faced with a threat of this magnitude by a foreign power, I would invoke the War Powers Act and mobilize all available military resources and request the Congress to declare a state of war. However, two factors unique to this situation make that an unwise choice. The first factor is that we are not just dealing with a foreign power but an alien power from another planet light-years away. If this became public, we would be looking at mass hysteria.

"Secondly, we have hundreds of thousands of unidentified enemy combatants mixed in with the world population and can't tell who the enemy is without DNA testing. For this reason, I find it not only necessary but also essential that the United States move unilaterally to extinguish this threat. I will be calling in the Joint Chiefs of Staff. I will have them sequestered while their DNA is processed. Once established that we have no ALFs among them, I will order them to have all military personnel tested starting with combat units. Anyone found to be an alien will be sent to the Guantanamo Marine Base in Cuba and held in detention. Once this is accomplished, we will begin mandatory screening of all civil service employees.

"We don't have time for diplomacy in shutting down those factories, and I am sure I will take plenty of heat for this, but tomorrow I will notify the countries involved that they have forty-eight hours to shut down the factories generating the chlorofluorocarbon emissions and the coal-burning power plants. As an incentive for a peaceful solution, I will offer financial aid to assist those countries who comply. But any factories still in operation when the deadline expires will be taken out militarily.

"Doctor, I would like you to work on finding a way to identify the aliens among us in a more expeditious way than DNA testing and get back to me as soon as possible with any breakthroughs in that area.

"Deputy Shore, you and Ms. Clift will be taken by helicopter to Andrews Air Force Base where you will board a C-130 transport to take you to our base in Ushuaia, Argentina. From there, you will be taken by helicopter to rendezvous with the USS *Hampton*. I am giving you these sealed orders to give to Captain Thayer. They instruct him to follow the coordinates you give him to the suspected location of the enemy's command post and make every attempt to open up a communications channel. If we can open up a dialogue with these people, we may be able to come up with some sort of mutually beneficial agreement and avoid further bloodshed. That would be my hope. Are there any questions?" asked the president.

Lyman stood up. "Mr. President, we have recently discovered, as a result of recent DNA testing, that the now deceased Mr. Mankewitz was an ALF. I believe he was part of a campaign by the alien command to keep us focused on the ozone depletion problem to the point where we would not realize what was happening in another area," said Lyman.

"Please continue, Deputy," said the president.

"Well, sir, it occurred to me that the one thing most important to the aliens is the air they are breathing. They are suffering from carbon dioxide deprivation. So I asked myself, What is the quickest way to increase the amount of carbon dioxide in the atmosphere?"

Hearing this, Dr. Emmons stood up and said, "The rain forests."

"Exactly," said Lyman. "There are six major rain forests in the world. The Amazon tropical rain forest and river basin is the largest of the six with approximately 390 billion trees. Hundreds of millions of metric tons of carbon dioxide are locked in these trees and their leaves, branches, and trunks. It is my belief that the aliens intend to somehow release that carbon into the air in the hope of making the air healthier for them and deadly for the human race. Such a huge release of CO_2 into the air would also drastically accelerate the process of global warming as it reaches the stratosphere, expanding the greenhouse effect. I think all of our immediate attention should be directed to the Amazon basin," Lyman concluded.

"This is quite a bombshell you are dropping on us on short notice or no notice at all, Deputy Marshal Shore. Does everyone here agree with the deputy's assessment of the situation?" asked the president.

Dr. Emmons answered first. "Mr. President, if he is right, then it is crucial that we move as soon as possible. While the emissions from the factories and fireplace chimneys are damaging the ozone layer, we have time to deal with those issues. But if the aliens find a way to release all of the carbon in the rain forests into the atmosphere, the effect on the human race would be quick and catastrophic," he said.

"Okay, I am going to set up an emergency meeting with the presidents of Brazil, Peru, Venezuela, Ecuador, Columbia, Bolivia, Surinam, Guyana, and French Guiana. I will apprise them of the situation and offer our assistance in a joint effort to protect this vast world resource. Deputy Shore, you will be going to Brazil to assist in coordinating the effort to determine what the aliens are up to and how to stop them. I will advise Captain Thayer to continue patrolling in the McMurdo area for the time being. This does not mean we are going to ease up on the pressure to have the factories shut down however. I will still be delivering the ultimatum to the leaders who have factories operating in their cities and countries, and I will be conferring with President Dubois to find out what progress the French are making," the president explained.

"For now, the rest of you just continue to exercise due diligence and accelerate your efforts to take these folks down. I have established a secure, encrypted email group, which includes only myself and those of you in this room, so we will be able to keep everyone in the loop regarding any developments going forward," the president said as he passed out slips of paper to each attendee with the information. "That concludes this meeting. Good day and thank you, all, for your devotion to your duty and your country."

When everyone left the Oval Office, the president stood looking out at the Rose Garden and pondered the fate of mankind.

Chapter 38

"I will be shutting down the factory today," said Victor Obano to his wife, Maria. "It is best for everyone." Victor had been watching the news on Nigerian television about President Chavez's ultimatum. While his government's official stand was one of defiance and denial, he knew shutting down the factory was just the right thing to do. His father would secure him a good government job, and as long as he continued to have access to tanks of supplemental carbon dioxide, he should be able to live a somewhat normal life and watch his daughters grow up. He would contact his counterparts in the other countries and encourage them to do the same and would advise Command of his actions and that he considers the mission a failure. "My father will be moving us to a safe location and will be providing security in the event that Command sends soldiers," he said as he ushered his family out of the house.

Chapter 39

Carlos Melendez had been saving pop-top beer and soda cans for several months until he had hundreds of them. In his home in Leticia, Colombia, he had two large tubs. One was filled with fine-powdered iron oxide, and the other with fine-powdered aluminum. He was filling the cans with one-quarter aluminum powder and three-quarters iron oxide and mixing them together. He would then insert an eight-inch strip of magnesium into the mixture and do the same thing with the next can. Each can would now be an incendiary thermite bomb and would be used to set fire to the Amazon basin. Water boils at 100 degrees Celsius, and napalm generates temperatures of 800 to 1,200 degrees Celsius. Thermite is more powerful than napalm. His fellow ALF soldiers were coming to his home daily, filling up their backpacks with these cans and leaving. ALFs in Manaus, Brazil; Coca, Ecuador; Iquitos, Peru; and Puerto Ayacucho, Venezuela, were doing the same thing out of their homes.

Command was coordinating the operation to send hundreds of these soldiers simultaneously from these locations into the Amazonian jungle to deposit and ignite their cans when the time was right. Global warming was already having the effect of warming the oceans, and at a certain point, this would lead to a drought in the Amazon basin. They needed to wait for the drought to dry out the rain forest to the point where these fires would be the most devastating and would spread through the entire basin, releasing vast amounts of carbon dioxide into the air and killing thousands of species of animal and plant life.

Chapter 40

Lyman Shore had just arrived at Manaus Air Force Base in Manaus, Brazil, where he would meet with the Brazilian base commander, Colonel Mauro Machuca. President Chavez had spoken to the presidents of all nine countries occupying the Amazon Rain Forest, and they had assured him of their complete support in finding and eliminating those who were sent to destroy the forest.

Now Lyman was addressing the colonel and his senior officers in the base commander's office. A US Army major fluent in Portuguese had traveled with him and was interpreting as he spoke.

"Colonel Machuca, on behalf of the United States government, I would like to thank you and your men for assisting us in facing this common threat. The United States Air Force is in the process of dropping hundreds of drones over all the entry points into the Amazon. Once done, the video feed will go to our people at Davis-Monthan Air Force Base in Arizona, where they will monitor it, and when potential targets are located, the information and location will be sent to us here so we can direct assets to eliminate the threat. We have forces from all nine countries owning real estate in the Amazon standing by," he said.

Two hours went by, then the video screen came on, and Captain Sara Huckabee was looking at them from Davis-Monthan AFB. "Gentlemen, the drones have been deployed. We have observed twenty individuals going to and coming from a resident in Manaus in the last hour and fifty or more entering the forest on foot. I am sending you the coordinates of the house and livestreaming the fifty on foot," she said.

"Thank you, Captain. Keep us posted," said Lyman.

Colonel Machuca got on the radio and ordered six Black Hawk helicopters to load up with ten Brazilian Marines each and head for the location where the fifty potential targets were entering the Amazon jungle. He also advised the local police to secure the residence.

The owner of the residence was filling cans when the police burst through his door and arrested him. The officer in charge called Colonel Machuca and reported the two tubs of unknown powder, and the colonel dispatched explosive experts to the house.

When the Black Hawks arrived at the coordinates, they observed fifty to seventy suspects wearing backpacks approaching the forest. Upon seeing the helicopters, they broke into a run for the safety of the jungle canopy. They were only an advanced group sent in to test the devices to determine how easy the magnesium strips would burn and for how long. The drought had not occurred yet, and the conditions were too wet for the forest to burn enough to obtain their objective. But when the Marines arrived, they panicked and ran. Three Black Hawks landed, and thirty Marines got out and ran in pursuit, while the other three helicopters flew deeper into the jungle, and the other thirty soldiers slid down ropes from the hovering choppers into the jungle and took up defensive positions in case the suspects were able to evade the pursuing Marines. The potential enemy was now caught between the two groups of Brazilian Marines and began to panic. Several of them stopped, took a can out of their backpack, and tried to light the magnesium strip. But the strip needs to be over an open flame for twenty to thirty seconds to ignite it, and time was something they did not have as the Marines closed in. They had only handguns but felt they had little choice and took up positions behind trees, trunks, and vegetation and fired on the pursuing soldiers. The Marines holding defensive positions heard the gunfire and radioed the pursuing force to coordinate their attack. The aliens were no match against the well-trained Marines with their assault rifles, and soon it was over. The backpacks and their contents were taken back to Colonel Machuca and Deputy Shore for examination.

Troops were sent into Leticia, Colombia; Coca, Ecuador; Iquitos, Peru; and Puerto Ayacucho, Venezuela, since these were the towns closest to or in the Amazon. During these searches, other home factories were found. All the homes in these towns were searched, and hundreds of these canned explosives were found and the residents taken into custody for DNA testing before being sent to Guantanamo. All nine countries involved with this operation would continue to be on high alert for any suspicious activity in the area from now on.

Chapter 41

Secretary General Antoine Laurent was monitoring operations as dozens of homes in Paris were being approached by police with warrants. Ozone-depleting chemicals were identified as being emitted from the chimneys of these homes, and strange fireplace inserts of a kind never before seen were found. Laurent ordered them to be sent in for analysis, and the entire families living in those homes were taken to detainment centers for testing and questioning. The French scientists had designed and built a portable device for detecting ODCs (ozone-depleting chemicals) and were in the process of getting these devices ready to be shipped to the other European countries once their leadership was briefed on the ALF threat. Soldier ALFs observed what was happening and reported back to the Command Center.

CHAPTER 42

With the rain forest threat handled for the time being, the president had a plane sent to Manaus to pick up Shore and fly him to the US Air Base in Argentina. He would reunite there with Linda Clift and be taken out by helicopter to rendezvous with Captain Thayer.

The USS *Hampton* had been patrolling the Antarctic area when it received orders to surface at a specific set of coordinates and take on two passengers.

"I understand you have orders from the president, Deputy Shore," said Thayer as he walked into his cabin, followed by Shore and Linda Clift.

"Yes, sir, Captain," replied Shore, handing the sealed envelope to him.

The captain sat down at his desk and opened the envelope and took a minute to read the contents. Then he put the orders in his desk and stood up and said, "Very well then. I suggest we proceed to the bridge where I will brief my first officer, and we'll be on our way."

Lyman and Linda listened and observed as the captain spoke with the FO, and the FO gave orders to set course.

Then one of the sailors took them to their separate quarters and told them how to get to the mess hall. Now they were sitting down at a small table, each with a hot cup of coffee in their hand.

"So tell me, Dr. Clift, let's suppose you've just saved the world from an alien invasion. What now?" said Lyman.

Linda smiled and said, "Well, Deputy Marshal Shore, I think you may be a little premature with the first part of that statement. But to answer the second part, I haven't the faintest idea."

"In that case," continued Lyman, "may I suggest San Antonio? It's a beautiful city with plenty to do, and who knows, maybe you'll meet someone special."

She looked Lyman straight in the eye for a few seconds. It was as if she were trying to figure out exactly who he was and if he was serious. "I'll tell you what, Deputy Marshal. Let's get this 'save the world' thing out of the way first, then we'll see," she finally said.

He just looked at her and said, "Fair enough. But just for the record, I think you're pretty amazing."

Just then, a sailor came in and walked over to their table. "The captain requests your presence on the bridge, folks," he said.

They got up, and Lyman replied, "Lead the way, sailor."

Working its way around a labyrinth of ice formations for the last hour, the *Hampton* was now arriving at its destination. Just two hundred yards ahead was the suspected location of the enemy's command post.

"Well, Deputy Shore, according to my eyesight and all of my very sophisticated instruments, there is nothing but water ahead of us," said Captain Thayer.

"Humor me, Captain," said Lyman. "Launch a probe out there and see how far it can go."

"Yeoman Sanders, do as the deputy suggests. Launch probe," Thayer responded.

"Yes, sir, Captain," responded Sanders as he followed orders.

They all watched through the forward observation screen as the probe moved slowly forward—one hundred yards, two hundred yards, two hundred twenty yards.

"Looks like just water, Deputy. You know what they say. If it looks like a duck, walks like a duck, and quacks like a duck, it's probably a—"

"Captain," interrupted Sanders, "the probe stopped its forward motion at two hundred forty-three yards out. It's as if it ran into a wall, but there is nothing there."

They're Here!!

"Well, I'll be damned," said Thayer. "Open all communications channels and ask whatever that is to identify itself."

"Yes, sir," Sanders replied.

CHAPTER 43

With Dorlestor gone, Captain ZReubnth was now in charge of the command post. He was watching the approach of the *Hampton* and monitoring its communications. Having recently received word about the setbacks in France and the Amazon, he was currently communicating with the High Council when the *Hampton* hailed him. While he had no weapons, he was not concerned. Nothing the *Hampton* could throw at it could penetrate the command post, which arrived on Earth as a spacecraft plunging into the ocean water and making its way to this location before transforming into the command post template and initiating the cloaking procedure—technologies not yet dreamed of by the inhabitants of this planet. His superiors back home on Veteris Orbis were monitoring recent events and ordered him to respond to the American attempts at communication. Dorlestor had gone silent and was declared missing in action. With their presence now known and the factories being shut down, their main concern now was the well-being of their people living on Earth. The two other planets they were preparing were progressing favorably, and Earth was no longer considered essential.

"This is Captain ZReubnth of the interplanetary vessel Scrutator from the planet Veteris Orbis. State your purpose," came through the speakers on the USS *Hampton*.

They're Here!!

"I'll be a son of a bitch," said a startled Captain Thayer. "This is Captain Frederick Thayer of the USS *Hampton*, and my purpose is to expedite your departure from this planet."

Just then, Captain ZReubnth uncloaked the ship, and suddenly, Captain Thayer and his crew were looking at what looked like a huge glass wall directly in front of them, encompassing three levels with perhaps one hundred people moving about on all levels, performing various tasks. On the top level in dead center, a man in a white uniform stood facing them. This was obviously who he was talking to.

"We have instructed all of our people to cease from all illegal activity and conduct no further violence against your people or infrastructure. We are prepared to leave your planet and will make no further attempts at altering your environment or weather patterns. We will, however, be leaving behind approximately five hundred thousand people. The vast majority of these people have been productive, honest, tax-paying citizens in every field of endeavor. We ask you to accept those individuals into your society without punishment. We also fully expect that those who have committed crimes will be prosecuted under your legal system. May we have your agreement that our people will be treated fairly?" asked Captain ZReubnth.

Captain Thayer stood there for a moment, absorbing what he had just heard, then looked at Shore. "What's your take on this, Marshal Shore?" he asked.

"Looks to me like we've become a bit of a thorn in their side and we've got a shot at ending this thing," said Lyman.

Thayer keyed the mike. "Your request will be relayed to our president. Please stand by," he responded.

One hour later, Thayer opened communication to the aliens again. "I have been instructed to tell you that we will treat those who have committed no crimes as we do all of our citizens and will encourage the leaders of other nations where they reside to do the same. There is one condition we require, however, and that is that you provide us with all of the names and current locations of your people. If you force us to track them down, then all bets are off," Thayer said.

"Agreed," said the captain. "Sending the information to you now. We require you to move your vessel to enable us to navigate to open water for our departure," Captain ZReubnth said as he began the process to revert to spacecraft.

Captain Thayer confirmed receipt of the email with attachment containing the information agreed to and ordered full reverse. As the sub moved slowly back, the crew witnessed the most amazing thing as the command post morphed from a square glass enclosure to a sleek, round spacecraft.

One hour later, the *Hampton* surfaced and watched the alien ship shoot out of the water and disappear from sight in seconds.

CHAPTER 44

In the next few days, President Chavez made an address before the United Nations in New York City, explaining the recent events and encouraging cooperation among all nations to treat the aliens fairly and provide them with medical care as needed and supplemental carbon dioxide. Scientists assured the population that without continued man-made chemicals entering the stratosphere, Earth would heal over time with ozone levels rising and global warming slowing down.

Dr. Emmons came up with a breathalyzer that would measure carbon dioxide. The average human exhales approximately 4 percent carbon dioxide with each breath since it considers it a waster product. The aliens, however, would want to retain the carbon dioxide and therefore register from 0 to 2 percent per exhale. These breathalyzers would be used to identify suspected aliens and made available to law enforcement everywhere.

CHAPTER 45

Drake Borden had numerous job offers to choose from but decided he would lay-low for a while and assess his options. He was in demand by the networks and cable news shows to do interviews and was going to just ride the tide for a little while. The governor and the DA in Austin had been taken into custody by the FBI, and a special election was called to fill the now vacant governor position.

Lyman Shore took some time off and invited Linda to visit him in San Antonio. He saw her standing there in the lower-level pickup area outside the baggage claim waiting for him and felt a kind of happiness he didn't think he would ever feel again.

"It's hotter than hell here," she said as she threw her bag in the open trunk.

"But it's nice and cool in the car, and everywhere we go will be air-conditioned. So what's the big deal, girl?" he said, closing the trunk and running to open the passenger's door for her.

She stopped and looked at him holding the door open for her and said, "Well, you're trying. I'll give you that, Deputy." And she got in.

He closed the door and walked around and jumped into the driver's seat. Linda let out a deep breath as she sank into the Camaro's leather seat, and Lyman planted his back against it as he took off.

"I just have a one-bedroom condo, so I hope you don't mind sleeping on the couch," he said playfully.

They're Here!!

"I'm sure we can work something out," she replied without looking at him.

He looked over at her and smiled. "Listen," he said, "I'm really glad you came and just want to spend some time with you without anyone shooting at us for a change. The bedroom is yours. I'll do just fine on the couch. It's not unusual for me to sleep there and leave the bedroom empty, so no need to feel bad. I thought we would go clean up and go to the Tower of the Americas for dinner. Are you game?" he asked.

"Sounds like fun," Linda replied.

When they got to the condo, they took the elevator up to the fourth floor. Lyman unlocked the door, and Linda walked in first. As he walked in behind her and turned to close the door, he saw a man standing behind the door, holding a gun on him. It looked to be a .40-caliber Glock 22, and the man was smiling.

"Hello, Lyman," he said.

"Do I know you?" said Lyman as he closed the door behind him.

"No, but I know you, Deputy Marshal. You're the guy who just wouldn't go away, wouldn't die. But you're gonna die now, and your girlfriend here will just be a bonus. You know, Jason really wanted to bone her," he said crudely. "But you made sure that didn't happen. I just wanted the satisfaction of seeing your face when you realize you're about to die at my hands. But now I get the added bonus of killing your girlfriend right in front of your eyes first."

Just then, someone banged on the door. "Hey, bro!" a voice yelled through the door.

Dorlestor instinctually whipped his head to the door, and at the same time, Lyman pulled out his 9 mm Glock 17 and fired two times at center mass. There was a shocked look on Dorlestor's face then nothing as the gun fell from his hand. He was dead before he hit the floor.

At the sound of gunfire, Gary kicked open the door with gun in hand. He looked down at Dorlester, who was facedown on the floor with the Glock 22 lying unfired next to his right leg. "Who's that?" he said.

"That, I believe, is what was behind door number 1," replied Lyman. Seeing the confused look on Gary's face, he said, "Nevermind, big brother. I will say, you could not have picked a better time to knock on my door. I do believe you may have just saved both of our lives. Tell you what. I'm gonna call my boss and have him send someone out to pick up our friend here. Then we are all gonna go crash a party."

Epilogue

The Tower of Americas is a San Antonio landmark. Perhaps not as widely known as the Space Needle in Seattle, but it stands 622 feet tall compared to the 604 feet of the Needle. At the top is a rotating restaurant where you can eat while enjoying a panoramic view of the city and the surrounding area for miles around.

Lyman, Linda, and Gary were just stepping off the elevator at the top and walking into the restaurant.

"Party of three?" inquired the receptionist.

"No," Lyman answered. "We'll be joining another party and might need to do some rearranging of tables." With that, Lyman walked over to a table seating a party of three. "May we crash this family outing?" he said to the older man with the crew cut.

David Emmons got up smiling and said, "You sure can, young man."

Jim and Julie also got up, and handshakes and hugs went around as introductions were made.

Everyone ordered dessert and coffee and talked about the craziness of the last few weeks. As Lyman was having a second cup of coffee poured, his cell went off with the caller ID showing Bret Boyer.

"What's up, ammo man?" said Lyman.

"I'm in real trouble, Shore," he said in a trembling voice. "Remember you said you were my go-to guy?"

About the Author

Kenneth A Kidd is currently living in Ocala, Florida, with his wife, Lyndell; two dogs, Atlas and Athena; and a cat. Born in Fall River, Massachusetts, Ken enlisted in the US Air Force in 1966, serving in Oklahoma, Guam, and California. He obtained the rank of staff sergeant before his honorable discharge in 1970. He has always had a love of acting beginning in high school plays and continuing on a part-time basis throughout his life.

He appeared in numerous local television commercials in various markets as well as voice-overs in markets in Shreveport, Louisiana. Ken appeared in the movie *The People vs. Larry Flynt* as a Cincinnati detective who arrests the Larry Flynt character played by Woody Harrelson. He was a police officer in Benton, Arkansas, and a private detective doing surveillance and accident investigation work. Ken and his wife lived in San Alejo, Ecuador, from 2012 to 2015 before moving to Florida. He has also enjoyed writing poetry and is currently working on a sequel to *They're Here!!*.

www.ingramcontent.com/pod-product-compliance
Lightning Source LLC
LaVergne TN
LVHW091933070526
838200LV00068B/907